FIRESTORMERS

Firestormers is published by
Capstone Young Readers,
a Capstone imprint
1710 Roe Crest Drive
North Mankato, Minnesota 56003
www.mycapstone.com

Cataloging-in-Publication Data is available on the
Library of Congress website.
ISBN: 978-1-62370-756-9 (paperback)

Summary:
As the climate changes and the population grows,
wildland fires increase in number, size, and
severity. Only an elite group of men and women
are equipped to take on these immense infernos:
FIRESTORMERS! Their gritty, life-or-death missions
are sure to make any reader sweat.

Printed in China.
009595F16

FIRESTORMERS

ELITE FIREFIGHTING CREW

written by CARL BOWEN
cover illustration by MARC LEE

Capstone Young Readers
a capstone imprint

FIRESTORMERS

ELITE FIREFIGHTING CREW

As the climate changes and the population grows, wildland fires increase in number, size, and severity. Only an elite group of men and women are equipped to take on these immense infernos. Like the toughest military units, they have the courage, the heart, and the technology to stand on the front lines against hundred-foot walls of 2,000-degree flames. They are the FIRESTORMERS.

KLAMATH NATIONAL FOREST

Established:
May 6, 1905
Coordinates:
41°30′01″N
123°20′00″W
Location:
California, USA
Oregon, USA

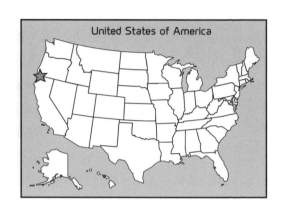

Size:
1,737,774 acres (2,715 square miles)
Elevation Range:
450–8,900 feet above sea level
Ecology:
Stretching from northern California into southern Oregon, Klamath National Forest is a rich, diverse biosphere. Stands of old-growth Ponderosa pine and Douglas fir dominate the landscape from the banks of the Salmon and Scott Rivers to the top of the Klamath mountains. Many threatened and endangered species call this region home, including northern spotted owls and wild coho salmon.

MAP

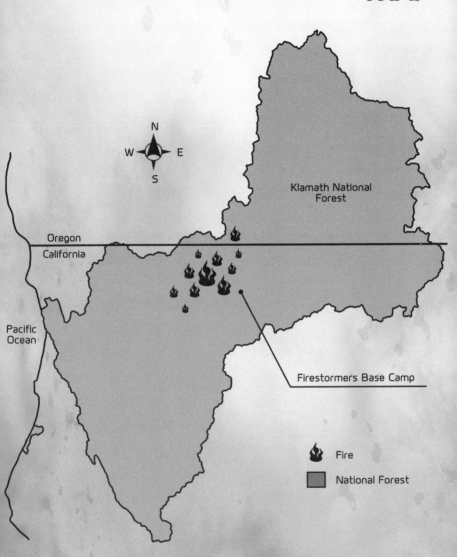

Klamath National Forest

Oregon

California

Pacific Ocean

Firestormers Base Camp

Fire

National Forest

CHAPTER ONE

Lieutenant Jason Garrett didn't consider himself a thrill seeker. He didn't consider himself a hero either, or even much of a leader. How then, he wondered, did he wind up inside a CASA 212 turboprop, ready to jump onto the fire front of a two-thousand degree inferno? It was enough to make him question his sanity.

Or maybe, he thought, *I'm just a closet adrenaline junkie.*

"Five minutes!" shouted the flight's jumpmaster as he worked his way through the plane's cramped passenger compartment.

The jumpmaster was a kid just out of college, who'd been hurling himself out of airplanes for a decade already. Lieutenant Garrett had it on good authority that the kid was the best in California. Still, Garrett would've preferred that someone older than himself perform the final checks on his crew's chutes and gear riggings.

Lieutenant Garrett would've also preferred to be on the ground, all things considered. He knew how to skydive — he'd been on dozens of training jumps — but this was his first jump as an official smokejumper. It was also his first mission as strike team leader for the nation's newest, most elite firefighting crew: Firestormers.

That fact alone should have made Garrett proud. It didn't. And his training should have overridden his nervousness. It hadn't.

As the plane neared its designated drop zone, Lieutenant Garrett couldn't help but wonder, *What the heck am I doing here?*

* * *

"Dad, what am I doing here?" Garrett had asked his father three months earlier.

Jason's father, Senator John "Big Jack" Garrett, had invited him to breakfast out of the blue. After working back-to-back, twenty-four-hour shifts at the Portland fire station, Jason would've preferred to sleep. But nobody said no to Big Jack.

"I talked to the governor yesterday," Big Jack said through a mouthful of thick-cut bacon. "He tells me you turned down a medal for what you did last week."

"You mean my job?" Jason asked. He hadn't eaten much of his own breakfast, which his father had ordered for him like he was a kid. "I don't want a medal for doing my job."

Big Jack slurped a forkful of sunny-side-up eggs. "You saved eighteen people's lives, son. Kids, even. Heck, you should be fighting off interviews from *Good Morning America*."

"It's just the job, Dad," Jason insisted. "Some days are better than others."

"Bah, you deserve it," Big Jack asserted. He looked around at the other patrons and announced, "This guy's a hero! And he's my son!"

Jason tried to sink into the diner's greasy floor.

The day his father was boasting about had been a good one, no doubt. Jason's station had received a call about a fire at Portland's largest high school. Most of the students and faculty had made it out, but a faulty alarm in the school's theater had failed to alert the drama club. Jason led a firefighting crew through the blaze and smoke to set them free.

Minutes afterward, dozens of videos of him helping the drama teacher limp to safety, surrounded by coughing, sweating student actors, surfaced on the Internet. The fact that the high schoolers were dressed for a production of *Cats* helped the video go viral overnight. The local news interviewed Jason — twice. Calls praising Jason's heroic act flooded the fire chief's office. The mayor even congratulated him personally.

"Let me ask you," Big Jack went on, picking up his sourdough toast and gesturing with it as he spoke. "Have you changed your mind about campaigning for me next year?"

Big Jack had been asking this whenever he was up for re-election for as long as Jason had been a firefighter. Jason always told him the same thing.

"You'll do just fine without me, Dad."

"Thought so," the senator said. "And since that's what I figured you'd say, let's talk about why I really wanted to meet you. How much do you know about the Forest Service?"

Jason blinked a few times, caught off guard. "Not much. It's a federal agency, right? Watches out for National Parks and stuff like that?"

"In a nutshell," his father confirmed. "They're the people most worried about wildland fires. They used to make those Smokey Bear commercials, remember?"

"Who?"

Big Jack shook his head in disappointment. "Before your time, I guess. Anyway, the Forest Service has a huge budget for fighting wildfires, but last year they blew through the money just two months into fire season. So they're trying something different. They're calling their new program the National Elite Interagency Wildfire Rapid Response Strike Force."

"That's a mouthful," Jason said. That went for the name as well as for the bite of toast his father insisted on chewing as he said it.

Big Jack burped. "The guy in charge calls them *Firestormers*. And right now he's recruiting the cream of the crop from fire services all over the West, looking for folks willing to fight these infernos wherever they pop up."

Jason's eyes narrowed. "And . . ."

"I submitted your name."

"What?" Jason exclaimed. "I don't know anything about fighting wildland fires. They're completely different from structure fires. I'm not trained for —"

"Relax, kiddo," Big Jack said. "They'll train you. Besides, it's just digging ditches, basically. It's hardly complicated."

Jason doubted that.

"The real work's done at the organizational level," Big Jack continued. "The folks who coordinate all the ditch digging and the bulldozing and whatnot — they're the ones doing the heavy lifting. It takes a keen mind, strong organizational skills, and leadership abilities. Everybody from your station's lieutenant all the way up to the governor's office agrees you've got all that in spades."

"Maybe because you told them to think that," Jason mumbled.

Big Jack shrugged, though he couldn't hide a wry smile. "Folks listen when I talk sense," the senator said, quoting his favorite campaign slogan. "And now I want you to listen. The Forest Service has appointed an old veteran fire chief out of California, Anna MacElreath, to head up this strike force. She's meeting with fire chiefs and local authorities in at-risk wildland areas. She's going to be here in Portland next week, and I want you to meet with her."

"Why?"

"Well, for one thing, as far as the family business goes, this is some great leadership experience."

"Family business? You mean politics?" Jason asked. "Pass."

"Not politics," Big Jack said, though that was clearly what he meant. "Community service. Besides, this is going to fast-track that promotion to lieutenant you've been waiting for. Also, you'd be a federal employee instead of a county firefighter. Better pay, better benefits, better union representation. Probably better equipment. And you'd get to travel regularly — at least from Arizona to Alaska."

Jason said nothing.

Big Jack stood, pulled a wad of cash from his back pocket, and threw half of it on his empty breakfast plate. "All I'm saying is this is good work that we all know you're capable of. Just meet with this chief, all right? Talk to her. See if joining the Firestormers is something you'd be interested in. I wouldn't want you to miss the opportunity, in case it turns out to be just right for you."

Jason sighed. "Okay, Dad," he said. "I'll talk to her."

"Attaboy!"

* * *

"We're over the drop zone, Lieutenant," the jumpmaster declared. He popped the seal on the turboprop's door and slid it open. Wind roared into the passenger compartment, silencing the Firestormers crew.

Lieutenant Garrett stood from his jump seat and walked toward the open door of the CASA-212. Five thousand feet below, eleven thousand acres of California's Klamath National Forest burned. Garrett felt the heat warm his face and the smoke sting his eyes.

Nobody says no to Big Jack, Garrett thought. Then he gave the jumpmaster a thumbs-up and looked back at his team.

Two dozen determined faces stared back at him expectantly. Lieutenant Garrett didn't know if they were waiting for his order, or if they wanted him to say something inspirational to commemorate the first Firestormers mission.

"Who wants to storm a fire?!" Garrett finally shouted over the turboprop's roaring engine. *Ugh,* he groaned to himself at the bad action-hero catchphrase.

Nobody moved or spoke. Big Jack's campaign slogan, "Folks listen when I talk sense," echoed in Garrett's ears, and he couldn't help but chuckle.

Just then, one of his crew bosses — Sergeant Heath Rodgers — stood, reached up, and banged a fist twice against the plane's low ceiling.

"Hoorah!" he called.

Jason smiled and repeated the gesture. "Hoorah!"

As one, each and every Firestormer did the same. Even the jumpmaster did it, grinning from ear to ear. "Hoorah!" they shouted in unison.

CHAPTER TWO

"There are times when I hate my job," Chief MacElreath said over the insistent buzzing of her cell phone. "Dinnertime, for example."

"Just answer the phone, Anna," her husband Brett said, rolling his eyes.

As the chief stood from the table, Brett took a bite of his steaming sloppy joe, mugging delicious bliss like he was auditioning for a TV commercial.

The chief pretended to ignore him. "MacElreath," she said into phone. "Uh-huh. How many acres now?"

"Hello, David," Brett called out from the table.

"He says, 'hi,'" MacElreath relayed. "He also apologizes for interrupting dinner."

Brett cocked an eyebrow. "Does he now?"

"No."

Chief MacElreath frowned, listening to what

the person on the line was saying, then asked, "How long? All right then. I'll get my stuff. See you in a bit. Okay, bye."

MacElreath ended the call and sighed.

"Where's this one?" Brett asked.

"Upstate," she said. "Klamath National Forest."

"How bad is it?" he asked.

"About eleven thousand acres. The team's already in the air."

Brett stood from the table. "I'll wrap up dinner."

"Thanks, hon," MacElreath said. "I got to get my bag."

* * *

Five minutes later, Chief MacElreath met David Holloway, her right-hand man, at the door. Holloway popped in briefly and gave Brett an apologetic shrug. "Dinnertime, huh?" he asked. "Sorry."

"It's the job," Brett said, shrugging back.

"She'll be back soon," Holloway told him. "A few days, probably. Maybe a week at most. Two weeks, tops." He laughed.

Brett couldn't help but chuckle along. "I know the drill," he said, grinning.

With that, Chief MacElreath and Holloway

headed out and piled into David's car. Holloway glanced back toward the front door, where Brett stood watching them pull away. "He doesn't like me much, does he?" he muttered.

"I'm lucky he even puts up with me." MacElreath said, blowing Brett a kiss goodbye.

"So how much do we know?" the chief asked, turning her attention back to Holloway. "About Klamath, I mean."

"Not much yet," Holloway said, his attention focused on the road. "It started out as lightning. Three separate incidents grew together and blew up. The wind's been fanning for it days. The local departments needed us."

"Who's in command on site?" MacElreath asked.

"A local captain," Holloway said. "He caught the first call and then took over for the other two incident commanders when his fire grew into theirs. His name's Pete Kinsey."

"Oh joy," MacElreath said without enthusiasm.

"You know him?" asked Holloway, curious.

"He'd just made lieutenant when I was a smokejumper out there. He's ambitious, popular up the chain of command but not down. Very career-focused, to put it politely."

"I'm sure rising in rank has mellowed him," Holloway suggested.

"No doubt," said the chief. "Besides, if he starts acting up, I'm going to pass him off to my liaison officer."

"Oh joy," Holloway said. He was MacElreath's liaison officer, after all.

"Have you talked to Tom and Smalls yet?" the chief asked, unwrapping the still-steaming sloppy joe on her lap.

"They should be waiting for us," Holloway said. "Thomas was already at the office when the call came in, and Sam lives closer than you and I do."

"Tom works too much."

"Don't we all?" Holloway suggested.

Chief MacElreath smiled ruefully, thinking of Brett at home.

* * *

As MacElreath finished her sandwich, they arrived at the newly formed Firestormers' headquarters. It wasn't much to look at. The Forest Service had set aside a suite of offices for the chief, her command staff, and their assistants. The smokejumpers, Hotshots, and other firefighters who made up the Firestormers' main workforce had a separate, off-site facility. The headquarters' only notable feature was the giant H in the center of the parking lot. Chief MacElreath and her people called it the Jump Point. And right now a helicopter was parked on it.

MacElreath and Holloway walked toward the helicopter, where the flight crew and the rest of the chief's command staff were waiting.

Thomas White, Chief MacElreath's safety officer, stood up straight as they approached. On the asphalt beside him sat a suitcase the size of a steamer trunk. Thomas worked long hours and hardly ever went home, which explained his perpetually scruffy look. MacElreath figured he'd probably skipped dinner altogether on this particular night. Samantha Smalls, the team's public information officer, stood beside him, looking quite the opposite: tough, smart, put-together. She reminded the chief of herself — maybe ten, twenty years ago. And next to her, Alan and Tonya Duncan polished off fast-food burgers, sharing them with the obedient fire dogs at their feet.

"Anybody heard from Mike or Tim?" Chief MacElreath asked as her staff gathered at the chopper.

"I have, Chief," Thomas said. "Mr. Farrant and Mr. Greer reported in. They're going to Klamath with the strike teams. They'll meet us there."

"All right then," said Chief MacElreath. "Let's load up."

* * *

Chief MacElreath had certainly seen larger fires, but that didn't mean much as she peered out the chopper's window from five thousand feet. The sun had yet to rise over Klamath National Forest. Skyscrapers of smoke billowed into the air, blotting out the moon and remaining stars. The blaze beneath oozed across the landscape with a hideous, gleaming magnificence. The flames grew hundreds of feet tall, whipping back and forth like dancing devils. This back-and-forth motion created a beat — a pulse — like glowing blood flowing through the veins of an invisible beast.

A beast MacElreath knew all too well.

The chief watched with a mixture of relief and regret as the helicopter turned away from the fire and started toward its final destination. The relief came from the sane, responsible part of her brain. The regret came from her fonder memories of being a young smokejumper.

Back then, she and twenty other firefighters would have kept flying toward the inferno and parachuted right on top of it, like her own Firestormers were doing at that very moment.

"Missing it?" Holloway asked from the seat next to the chief. He too, MacElreath noted, was staring out the window with longing. Holloway had been part of a Hotshot crew when he was younger, doing the same nasty work the chief's smokejumpers had done, without the plane ride.

"Maybe a little," MacElreath told him. "Pretty crazy, right?"

"Maybe a little," Holloway replied.

"You two having a midlife crisis?" Samantha Smalls asked, grinning at them from the other side of the chopper.

"Midlife?" Holloway said. "I wish. I'd love to make it to a hundred and eighteen."

"No comment." Chief MacElreath smiled.

A short time later, the chopper set down on a Forest Service airfield, about one hundred miles from the blaze. Three helicopters were already parked there, as well as two red and white CASA-212 airplanes with the Firestormers' logo painted on the tails. A barracks had been built into one of the unused hangars. The Firestormers, as well as other Hotshot and smokejumper crews, would stay there while off duty — if they ever were off duty, that is.

MacElreath's operations section chief Michael Farrant and planning section chief Tim Greer greeted her on the tarmac. They directed everyone to the awaiting Forest Service SUVs.

"Mike," MacElreath said, shaking her op sec's hand. "Got everybody up in the air?"

"They should be dropping out of it right about now," Farrant confirmed.

MacElreath shook her planning chief's hand as well. "Tim. Got a report for me?"

"I always do, ma'am," Greer said, gesturing to the laptop computer tucked under his arm. Chief MacElreath took it from him carefully and made for the SUVs. Her staff followed, splitting up between the two vehicles.

"Where's the Incident Command Post?" the chief asked as Greer got behind the wheel.

"Wilmond High School," Greer replied. "The town's been evacuated, so we've got the place to ourselves. The locals should have it set up now."

"Just in time for us to kick them out," Holloway said, taking a seat next to the chief. "That's always a fun conversation."

"I'm glad I'm not the liaison officer who's got to have that talk," Chief MacElreath teased.

"If it gets hairy," Holloway began, "I'll just hide behind you and let you sort it out."

Chief MacElreath laughed. Right now, she'd take any laugh she could get it. They all had long, hard days ahead of them, she knew. In a few hours, none of them were going to feel much like laughing.

"All right then," the chief said, buckling herself into the SUV and then opening Greer's laptop to read the preliminary reports of the fire. "Let's get on with it."

CHAPTER THREE

Let's get on with it, thought Lieutenant Garrett, standing at the open door of the CASA-212.

Garrett swallowed hard and leapt from the plane. Behind him, twenty-five men and women followed, and together they fell toward the devilish inferno below.

Growing up in downtown Portland, Garrett had never actually seen a wildland fire up close. His training had given him an idea of the scale and scope of such events, but nothing had prepared him for the inferno's raw power.

Lieutenant Garrett pulled his chute's ripcord and — *FWOOSH!* — the rushing air grew silent, replaced by the hideous roar of the fire below.

Across the horizon, he saw flames eating at the hills like a hungry dragon. White-orange tendrils swirled from the forest's undergrowth to the tops of the tallest trees. Smoke blackened the sky in all directions, piling up into the beginnings of a nearby thunderhead.

Suddenly, Lieutenant Garrett's chute pulled him off course, awakening him from the awe-inspiring scene. He looked around. Other Firestormers struggled with their chutes as well, fighting desperately to steer back toward the drop zone. If his crew landed outside of it, Garrett knew they'd have to struggle uphill before they could get to work. But he didn't want to land too close to the fire either, for obvious reasons.

Convection currents, Lieutenant Garrett thought. He'd never experienced them firsthand, but he'd read about them in his training manuals.

As the fire burned, it hurled superheated air upward. This rising hot air caused surrounding cooler air to flow inward and take its place, which the fire then heated and pushed upward and away again. This churning cycle of convection stirred intense, unpredictable winds this close to the blaze.

Garrett grabbed the parachute's steering lines and pulled on them like his life depended on it. Because it did. The lines tore through his Kevlar gloves, but Garrett managed to stabilize his chute.

Soon, he and the other Firestormers were on the ground in Klamath National Park — a mere five hundred yards from the fire front.

Garrett unhooked his chute and gathered it up as quickly as he could. He then made his way to a hilltop while his team pattered down around him. Garrett stared the fire in its beastly face and tried not to gulp like a cartoon character. Seeing the fire from the sky was one thing; looking at the blaze on its own level was worse. He felt like an ant that fancied itself a dragon slayer.

That, however, was what his training was for.

* * *

Those training weeks had been the most nightmarish, demanding, and rewarding of Lieutenant Garrett's life. Covering topics such as skydiving, primitive survival, geography, meteorology, emergency care, and fire science, the training had expanded his mind and toughened his body faster than he'd thought possible. His PT stats and technical proficiencies had earned praise from his instructors and impressed Chief MacElreath. He'd even earned the respect of his fellow trainees — some of whom had years of wildland experience.

By the end of the training, Garrett was a standout candidate, easily at the top of his class. Chief MacElreath had not only assured him that she wanted Garrett on her new strike force, but she'd given him a position as a strike team leader. The force had one strike team at the moment, consisting of four crews of five people each, plus Garrett and four auxiliary rangers. That Garrett had been given command of that team had not gone over well with everyone, but Chief MacElreath made it clear that she felt Garrett was the best person for the job. The others would just have to swallow whatever misgivings they might have and do the job they'd been hired to do.

Digging his radio out of a belt holster, Garrett keyed it to the plane's frequency and called to the onboard crew.

"Air Ops One, this is Strike One," he said.

"Go ahead, Strike One."

"We're down and secure," Garrett reported. "Ready for cargo."

"Roger that," the pilot replied. "Give us a ping."

Lieutenant Garrett dug a high-tech computer tablet out of his cargo pants, removed his torn gloves, and swiped the touchscreen. A handful of digital icons appeared in a cluster. Garrett tapped the one marked JPADS, and a topographical map of the drop zone appeared on the screen. Markers showed the position of Garrett's strike team and the CASA-212 above.

"Ping," Lieutenant Garrett said over the radio.

"Yeah, we got it, Strike One," the pilot said, making Garrett feel silly for pointing out the obvious. "Cargo's away. Good luck."

"Thanks."

At that, the CASA-212's marker banked away on the tablet's screen and markers representing the cargo arced toward the ground.

Lieutenant Garrett glanced up in time to see the actual plane turning away as large bundles dropped out of the back. As the packages fell, red and white parafoil chutes blossomed above them, slowing their descent.

Lieutenant Garrett turned his attention back to his tablet, considering how best to remotely guide the cargo to where his team could reach it.

The technology that allowed him to do so was called the Joint Precision Airdrop System. It consisted of two systems developed by the Army and Air Force. The first included satellite-linked weather tracking and global positioning systems that allowed the packages to track their relative position to the impact point. The second system included decelerator lines on the sides of the parafoils to cause drag. Applied with precision, that drag forced the parafoils to change direction in midair. Working together, the JPADS units could track where the packages were supposed to land and force them back in the right direction if wind blew them astray.

From his tablet, Lieutenant Garrett could have controlled the flight remotely by hand, but he decided to trust the computer to get the job done. That was what it was for, after all.

While waiting for the cargo to touch down, Lieutenant Garrett shrugged out of his rigging and stowed the parachute inside. As he was finishing that, Sergeant Heath Rodgers, one of his four crew bosses, joined him on the hilltop.

Lieutenant Garrett didn't know much about Rodgers, except that he'd been in the Marine Corps before moving back home to Arizona and becoming a firefighter.

Sergeant Rodgers didn't say anything. He seemed to be waiting for Garrett to talk first.

"Heath?" Garrett asked, glancing up from his computer tablet. The cargo was almost down.

"You planning to do your head count, Lieutenant?" the Marine veteran asked. "I figure Chief MacElreath is probably waiting to hear from us."

Garrett winced. He was supposed to have confirmed that everyone on the strike team had made the jump successfully and safely. He should have done it before he'd radioed for the cargo drop. Now he wasn't sure what to do. Finish monitoring the cargo drop that he'd already called for? Pass the tablet off to Sergeant Rodgers? Delegate the head count to Rodgers?

"Um . . ." Garrett hesitated. "I got ahead of myself, Rodgers. Do you think you could —"

"Already did," Rodgers said, his eyebrows pinched in a frown. "Count's good. All jumpers accounted for. No injuries. Want me to call it in?"

Lieutenant Garrett considered letting him, but it wasn't exactly protocol. The next person up in the chain of authority would be expecting to hear from the strike team leader, not one of the random crew bosses from the team.

"I'll take care of it," he said. "For now, I want you to round everybody up on this hill so we can set up camp and I can hand out assignments."

"Shouldn't we get the gear first?" Rodgers

asked, nodding toward Garrett's tablet. "We might need that to make camp."

Lieutenant Garrett felt his ears redden. *What am I thinking? Of course we need the gear first*, he thought.

Sergeant Rodgers's gaze was making him nervous. The Marine wasn't scowling at him, exactly, but he looked like he was trying very hard not to. It occurred to Garrett that Rodgers had several years of wildland firefighting under his belt. Lieutenant Garrett — with none to speak of — wasn't making a great impression of his alleged leadership skills.

"Right, right," he said. "Tell you what, round up your crew, Rodgers. Gather the gear up where it's touched down and bring it here. We'll set up on this hilltop and go from there."

Rodgers's almost-scowl deepened a little into an honest frown. "Wouldn't it make more sense for us to go to where the gear is and set up camp near there? That's assuming it's not closer to the fire than we are, of course."

"Yeah, no, it isn't," Garrett confirmed, feeling more foolish with every word. He checked his computer tablet again, seeing that the cargo had touched down about a hundred yards behind them. "No, it's farther out. That's a good idea. Let's do that."

"All right," Sergeant Rodgers said. The sour look on his face didn't go away. "I'll start rounding people up." He walked away, calling to his crew and to the other firefighters nearby.

Lieutenant Garrett descended the hill behind him with the tablet in hand. "That could've gone better," he mumbled to himself.

A guy like Heath Rodgers was used to the disciplined command and competent professionalism of the Marine Corps. Lieutenant Garrett, thus far, hadn't made a great showing of either. If he kept this up, the lieutenant feared, he'd only be proving right the misgivings some of the experienced firefighters had about him. But looking like a rookie for a moment wasn't quite as bad as the consequences of failing — namely, losing control of this wildfire.

Lieutenant Garrett needed to prove that he could get the job done. He needed to prove that he deserved to be in charge.

CHAPTER FOUR

"I'm in charge," Chief MacElreath told Captain Pete Kinsey.

They stood outside Wilmond High School, which had become a hive of activity. As the designated Incident Command Post for the Klamath fire, it was the central hub for all personnel heading up the firefighting effort. That included the acting incident commander, Captain Kinsey, the man currently in charge.

"You're the feds?" Kinsey asked. He was a tall, broad-shouldered man in his early forties, with prematurely gray hair. A distractingly well-styled mustache decorated his upper lip, gleaming with pasty-white wax. The shape of it deepened the frown on his face.

"Division Chief Anne MacElreath of the U.S. Forest Service. I'm with —"

"You're with those barnstormers," Captain Kinsey said, well aware. The two men behind him snickered on cue.

"Firestormers," Holloway corrected. Kinsey barely flicked him a glance. Backing down, Holloway produced his smartphone from his pocket and stepped away to make a call.

"The National Elite Interagency Wildfire Rapid Response Strike Force, to be exact," Chief MacElreath continued. "I'm taking over as incident commander. This is the operations section chief Michael Farrant. You'll be reporting to him for your deployment orders."

"Operations?" Kinsey asked, annoyed. "I was told this was to be a unified command at —"

"Let me just stop you," said Chief MacElreath. "You're going to tell me you got here first and started organizing the response to this fire, which makes this your command. We both know I outrank you."

"The Forest Service —" Kinsey began.

"— the Forest Service doesn't have this kind of authority," MacElreath finished for him. "Last year, before the election, you would have been right. But we've got a new president and a new power structure for certain federal agencies —

mine included. I can take this fire away from you, and that's what I'm doing."

"Well, then I'll have to see —"

MacElreath interrupted Kinsey with a laugh. "Let me guess." she said, "You want to see the paperwork relieving you of command."

"That's what you feds like, isn't it? You *love* your paperwork. I don't think I could step down unless everything was nice and official." Captain Kinsey smirked.

"Then you'll be glad to know there's a huge stack waiting for you back at your home station. We had it dropped off with your chief on our way here. If you want, pop on over there and see where he signed them all."

"Bull," Kinsey said in disbelief.

MacElreath smiled at him and glanced at her liaison officer. "Holloway," she prompted.

At her command, Holloway stepped forward and held out his smartphone to Captain Kinsey. "It's for you," he said. "Chief Barnes."

Kinsey took the phone, said a few words, and then went quiet. Finally, with a halfhearted "Yessir," he handed the phone back to Holloway.

"What'd he say?" asked Samantha Smalls, standing nearby.

Kinsey gritted his teeth. He glared at MacElreath and bit out, "If you come this way, I'll show you to your office. Chief."

* * *

Chief MacElreath's office, the heart of her Incident Command Post, turned out to be the Wilmond High School principal's office. It was as basic as it could be, with painted cinder block walls, a fiberboard drop ceiling, and an old warhorse of a metal desk that had been serving duty since the late eighties. A few inspirational cat posters on the wall encouraged MacElreath to "Hang in There!" and "Dream Big!" Hastily tacked-up maps of the local area decorated the remaining wall space, each covered in Captain Kinsey's handwritten notes.

"I was just getting set up," Kinsey explained, lingering in the doorway.

The rest of Chief MacElreath's team moved to their own work areas, taking over the teachers' lounge and the computer lab down the hall. MacElreath knew she'd be spending most of her time out among them, but she wanted to get acquainted with her own workspace first.

Kinsey was not making that easy.

"I've got this, Captain," MacElreath told him.

"Well, here," Kinsey said, trying unsuccessfully to slide around her and get into the office. "Let me just show you where I've marked — "

"I know where the fire caches are," the chief said. "I know where the responding stations are. I know where the staging areas are. I know where the airbase is. This isn't my first fire, Captain."

Kinsey flinched, taken aback.

"You want to make yourself useful?" MacElreath continued. "Report in with Chief Farrant. He'll have your assignments ready."

The captain turned without a word and stalked off down the hall.

Chief MacElreath shook her head. By all reports, Captain Kinsey was a competent firefighter and leader. He had the political savvy to make chief someday, if he wasn't such a pain to work with. Unlike Kinsey, most firefighters — from the rookies to seasoned chiefs — respected their places in the hierarchy of the Incident Command System.

The ICS had been modeled on the command structure of the U.S. Navy in the sixties and then modified by Arizona's state fire services. Decades later, fire services across the country had adopted the Incident Command System to streamline their chains of authority on any fire incident — from a garbage-can fire to a thousand-acre wildfire. During a blaze, the incident commander's subordinates presented up-to-the-minute information on the fire. Based on this info, the incident commander decided how best to battle the blaze. The subordinates then passed down those orders to their assistants, local staff, and strike team leaders on the ground. The team leaders relayed the orders to their crew bosses, who finally passed them to firefighters.

Authorizing the Forest Service to head up the Incident Command Structure was a relatively new procedure, born from the president's surprisingly robust environmental policy. It wasn't so new, however, that Captain Kinsey had any right to act surprised by it. Chief MacElreath's newly formed Firestormers program had been making headlines for months, after all. More likely, Kinsey's attempts to maintain control were purely political. Big-time wildfires reached big-time news outlets. A well-fought fire could turn an incident commander into a local celebrity. An ambitious, career-minded man like Kinsey would no doubt find that attention hard to resist.

"You going low-tech on us all of a sudden, Chief," a voice said from the doorway behind her.

Chief MacElreath turned and saw Samantha Smalls standing in the doorway, pointing at the wall of paper maps and Post-it Notes.

Chief MacElreath turned and saw Samantha Smalls standing in the doorway, pointing at the wall of paper maps and Post-it Notes.

MacElreath chuckled. "Kinsey's stuff," she explained.

"Good. Because the Wi-Fi network should be connected at any moment," Smalls reported. "When it is, I've got the standard boilerplate press release done and ready to send off. I also updated CAL FIRE and InciWeb, and I was fixing to update our Facebook and start sending out tweets."

"First of all, good job," said the chief. "Second — 'fixing'?"

Smalls smiled. "Didn't I say it right?"

"It's fixin'," MacElreath replied, emphasizing the Southern accent that even a decades-long career in California hadn't quashed completely. "And don't say fixin'. You're from New York. That's our word. In this job, you have to be yourself — and be your best self, at that."

Chief MacElreath caught herself sounding unusually preachy. Still, it was advice she wished she'd have gotten decades earlier as the nation's first female smokejumper.

"Lots to learn, I guess," Smalls said.

"Well, hang in there," MacElreath offered, pointing at the cat poster on the wall beside her that inspired the same message.

Smalls laughed.

"All right, back to work," ordered Chief MacElreath. "Set me up that press briefing for nine, and make sure we've got room for the reporters who want to stay with us and ride this out."

"Will do," Smalls said, saluting.

"Then try to eat something. It's going to be a long day, I reckon."

"I *reckon* you should too, Chief," replied Smalls, failing at another Southern accent.

Chief MacElreath smiled. "I will," she confirmed. "After I hear from Lieutenant Garrett and his crew. They should've set up camp by now. Then I'll review the incident reports and plug into WIMS to double-check the forecasts. Oh, and I need to go over your IAP again, and —"

"So I'll see you in the cafeteria sometime next week?" Smalls joked, then turned and left.

Chief MacElreath stared back up at the wall of paper maps and Post-it Notes.

No guarantees, she thought.

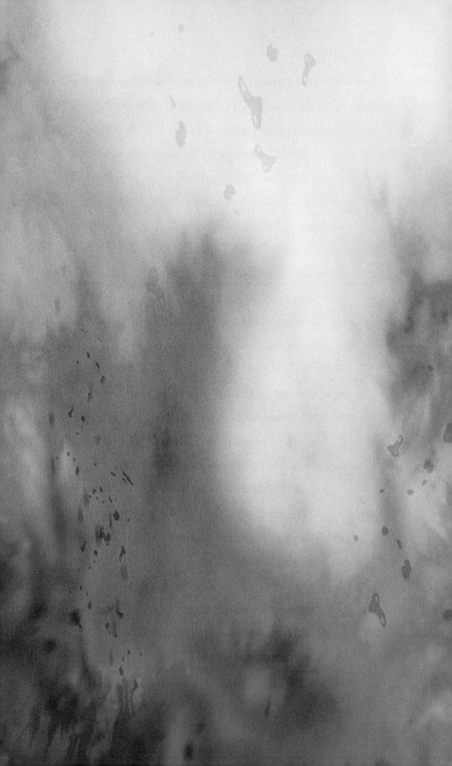

CHAPTER FIVE

"Yes, Chief, I guarantee it," Lieutenant Garrett said before switching off his two-way radio. He'd just guaranteed Chief MacElreath a zero-casualty mission and immediately regretted it. He knew — and he knew that she knew — that there were no guarantees in wildfire fighting.

Garrett shook off the statement and gathered his strike team around the spot where the cargo bundles had landed. Then he turned to his crew bosses. "Break down the crates," he commanded. "Start distributing crew gear."

Most of the gear in the cargo drop was camping supplies of one variety or another: tents, bedrolls, water, a generator, a folding camp stove, electric lanterns, toilet paper. Basically everything the team would need to weather a night in the wild. The crates also included heavy-duty chain saws, as well as drip-torches and all the gas and oil required to operate them. Each team was issued a pump-operated, shoulder-mounted bladder bag capable of carrying five gallons of water. The last bit packed down on the final pallet was a bundle of replacement handles for the hand axes, shovels, fire rakes, and other hand tools the team would employ on the fire line.

The Firestormers had jumped with a full kit of personal work and protective gear as well. Their uniforms were simpler than the bunker gear Lieutenant Garrett was used to wearing into a burning building. Bunker gear consisted of heavy boots, a thick jacket and pants, an air tank, a respirator mask, and the traditional "metro" style fire helmet. Working long hours outdoors would've been impossible in such heavy clothing, however, so wildland firefighters preferred simpler, lighter garb. They wore lightweight Nomex shirts and tear- and fire-resistant cargo pants. Their boots were heavy-duty logging boots of tough leather with chain-saw-resistant steel caps in the toes. On their heads they wore basic construction-style hard hats.

Already the crew had dumped the chute rigging and cargo webbing with which they had carried their individual gear. The less they took with them to the fire line, the longer they'd be able to work before exhaustion set in.

As for the gear they would be carrying, it was all surprisingly low-tech. The systems in place to guide the firefighting effort were state of the art, but the means of actually fighting the fire were quite the opposite. The Firestormers' main weapons against the blaze were chain saws for clearing trees, and hand tools, such as Pulaski axes, shovels, and sturdy fire rakes.

Also among the Firestormers' kit were several bottles of water and a single plastic-wrapped meal of high-energy, high-salt food for lunch. These military-style rations were called "meals, ready to eat" or MREs. Each firefighter also carried a first-aid kit and an emergency fire shelter. Nobody looked forward to a situation that required them to use those last two things.

While the crew bosses distributed the gear, Lieutenant Garrett and the strike team rangers set camp as quickly as they could. The remote command center would serve as the lieutenant's base of operations while he coordinated with Chief MacElreath at Incident Command. It was where he'd call the team back for dinner.

It was where everyone would sleep if their efforts required them to stay in the field for more than a day.

Once the basic structure of the camp was in place, Lieutenant Garrett called his crew bosses, their crews, and his rangers together at the center. He plugged his high-tech tablet into a small, portable projector. At once, the image from his tablet leapt onto the tent's canvas wall. The image showed a satellite photo of the forest before the fire began.

"Well, here we are," Lieutenant Garrett said. "Beautiful and scenic Klamath National Forest, not too many miles from the Oregon border."

Wavy contour lines covered the topographical map like a giant fingerprint. Steep hills and thickly wooded terrain dominated the geography.

The nearest residents were miles from this command post and roads didn't stretch out this far into the wild. That was why the strike team parachuted in rather than driving or walking overland. If the fire had been burning close to a usable road, Incident Command could have deployed engines and water tenders, or even bulldozers to manage the landscape and contain the flames. If the fire had been slightly farther from the roads but over less steep and awful terrain, Garret's strike team could have driven by buggy and then carried their gear on foot like a Hotshot crew.

While recruiting the Firestormers, Chief MacElreath insisted that its members cross-train as both Hotshots and smokejumpers, so they could deploy where they were needed most. This time, conditions called for an airdrop.

"Anyway," Lieutenant Garrett went on, "let's map out our fire. Our best estimates judging from local weather patterns suggest the fire started from lightning strikes, right around here." He pointed to a red, flashing dot on the projector image. "Six o'clock last night is when the calls started coming in to local fire stations about the smoke people could see from their homes."

Decades ago, the Forest Service relied on forest rangers stationed in watchtowers to keep an eye out for smoke from wildfires. These days, however, budget cuts had stripped those towers of their workers. But at the same time, cell phones and social media widened the net of watchful eyes, especially on the borders of the wildlands. By the time a fire got big enough to pose a danger to the surrounding forest, it threw up enough smoke and ash for someone to notice and call in. Whether that someone was a resident at the edge of the forest or a hiker on a trail, they got word to local departments, which let the Forestry Service know what was happening. And now, the evolving procedure was to let Chief MacElreath know, so she could get the Firestormers in on the action.

"Before convection forces got involved," Garrett continued, "the wind was blowing southwest steadily enough to push the fire east-northeast. By the time we got eyes on it and were able to map it, the fire had spread out like this."

Lieutenant Garrett pressed an icon on his tablet and updated the projected map. The highlighted area covered more than a thousand acres. Steady winds and ample fuel allowed the fire to spread over the terrain in an even pattern. From the point of origin, it spread east-northeast in a bulging, teardrop shape. No wildfire burned so evenly for long, however, especially over such hilly and uneven terrain. Fire flowed over a landscape like water — not downhill, exactly, but seeking out paths of least resistance.

Garrett pressed another icon on his tablet. "And this is our most recent report," he said as the map changed again. The image that took its place looked like an oak leaf. All around the perimeter of the fire front, individual tendrils of flame reached out from the main body like fingers spreading out from a hand. "These are what we're here to fight," Lieutenant Garrett said, trying to pump up his crews. "If we cut off these fingers, we can contain this fire and let it burn itself out before it puts any lives or property in danger."

He looked away from the screen, hoping to see two dozen inspired faces ready to get to work. Instead, he saw a bunch of bored men and women staring at him impatiently.

"Is this going to take long, Lieutenant?" Rodgers asked. "There's still *some* forest left."

A few firefighters chuckled at that. All of them were from Rodgers's crew. Most of the other firefighters hid their amusement. One of his other crew bosses, Chris Richards, ignored the comment altogether. The third, Michael Raphael, rolled his eyes. The last, Sergeant Amalia Rendon, frowned and cast a disapproving glance at Rodgers.

"Right, right," Lieutenant Garrett said. He tried not to let the comment rattle him, but he could feel his ears redden again. "Anyway, these are the deployment points around the fire. All strike teams should be in position now."

After another couple of taps on his tablet, a handful of green dots appeared at evenly spaced points around the fire's perimeter. Each one marked a strike team deployed on Chief MacElreath's orders to a point of attack near the largest fingers of the fire.

"This is us," Lieutenant Garrett continued, tapping one of the dots.

The other green dots represented local firefighters deployed from their own stations to contain isolated fires nearby. None of them, Garrett noticed, were as deep in the wilderness or as close to the ever-moving fire front as the Firestormers.

"Our job's simple," he said. "We're going to lock down the fingers of this fire as quickly as possible. Chief MacElreath is counting on us to keep the fire from spreading to the isolated fires that the locals have almost contained."

"Any idea who's working the isolated fires?" Sergeant Rodgers interrupted.

The question caught Garrett off guard. "Huh? Um, I'm not . . ." He tapped his tablet a few times and scratched his head. "No, it doesn't say here. Why?"

"If we're going to be watching their backs,

we should know if we can rely on them to be watching ours," Rodgers explained.

Lieutenant Garrett frowned in frustration. "Well, judging by the terrain it'll have to be a Hotshot crew. The fire's too far off roads for dozers, engines, or tenders. They're locals so they know the area. They managed eighty-percent containment of the isolated fires, so they're pretty good. Add that to the fact that Chief MacElreath let them stay where they are after she decided where to send us. I guess if you trust the chief's judgment, you can safely assume this Hotshot crew's going to be just fine watching your back. Any more questions?"

The Firestormers looked on, not saying anything.

"Okay then," said Garrett, wrapping up his pregame speech. "Let's get this done."

Lieutenant Garrett had expected those words to sound more stirring than they had. *Maybe I should quit wasting time pumping these people up and just get on with the details,* he thought. After all, this work probably seemed more commonplace for them than it did for him. This was his first wildfire — his first command. He was the only one out here with something to prove. Everyone else was just doing their job. They didn't need inspiration. They were professionals.

Lieutenant Garrett found himself gritting his teeth. He was embarrassing himself.

Fortunately, Sergeant Amalia Rendon came to his aid. With no trace of judgment or boredom or disappointment on her face, she stepped forward and cleared her throat to get Garrett's attention. "Sounds good, Lieutenant," she said. She gave him a reassuring, respectful nod. "Where's the anchor, and what's the plan?"

Lieutenant Garrett took a deep breath and let his mind shift gears. It was the sort of question he'd been trained to think through.

When he spoke earlier with Chief MacElreath, she had suggested where the strike teams might anchor their fire lines. But rather than giving Garrett a direct assignment of where to start, she'd encouraged the lieutenant to review the maps and aerial photos for himself.

"All right," Lieutenant Garrett said, isolating and enlarging a section of the map on his tablet. "As you can see here, there's a rocky canyon due south. That'll make a perfect natural firebreak. We'll start our line there and cut east-northeast up to Strike Two's anchor at the quarry."

He shrunk the map back down and used a stylus to draw a rough line from point to point. Rather than drawing a straight line, he traced the topography as best he could to most accurately represent the path his team would take.

"That line's about a mile longer than it needs to be," Rodgers piped up, unasked. "You've got it anchored behind the wind, and its tail edge curves out too far from the fire front before it joins up with Strike Two."

"Scared of a little extra hard work, Heath?" Sergeant Rendon said, smirking at him in a not-unfriendly way.

Sergeant Rodgers took her ribbing, but it didn't change his distaste for the lieutenant's proposed fire line. "Hard work's one thing, Amalia," he said, "but you know what kind of time frame we're dealing with. This kid's giving up acres of forest, and he's going to grind us into the ground trying to get this line dug on Chief MacElreath's schedule."

Lieutenant Garrett ground his teeth now. It was bad enough making *himself* look like a rookie with an uninspirational speech. He didn't need Rodgers actively undermining his authority on top of that.

"Hey," he snapped, putting a gravelly edge in his voice. Silence fell. Rodgers actually flinched at the interruption. "That's '*Lieutenant* This Kid' to you, Heath."

Garrett locked eyes with Rodgers and then grinned to stick a pin in the bubble of tension. Everyone relaxed. A few of the veterans chuckled and nodded approvingly at the lieutenant. Rendon gave a surprised snort of laughter.

"Fair enough," Rodgers said, backing down. "But do you at least see my point about the line?"

"This fire's moving and growing fast," Lieutenant Garrett said, "and the winds are unpredictable. If they shift and push this finger backward, I want it running up against that canyon and stopping. If we leave a gap back there and it gets in behind us, it's almost all uphill to this spot we're standing on."

This drew a few murmurs from the firefighters. Wildfires moved faster uphill than downhill. A fast-moving flame behind them — however unlikely — would have been a serious problem.

"As for the tail end," Lieutenant Garrett continued, "yeah, that balloons out a bit. At the fire's current growth rate, it's not going to be anywhere near that by the time we link up to

Strike Two's anchor. But you know better than I do how unpredictable fire is. If the fire front starts running before we get near that quarry, you're going to be glad for the extra distance between you and it."

Rodgers frowned thoughtfully but offered no further protest. More importantly, the other firefighters and crew bosses were nodding along, seeing the sense in the lieutenant's cautious line.

"As far as the plan of attack goes," Lieutenant Garrett said, breathing a little easier, "we'll keep it simple since this is our first time out. We'll do a bump-and-jump, short legs, maximum twelve-hour shifts."

Heads nodded all around, taking in the information.

"All right, class dismissed," Garrett joked, winning polite chuckles. "Crews, get your gear ready. Make sure you have everything you need. Rangers and crew bosses stick around. I'll give you your specifics."

The majority of the Firestormers backed off to perform one last check of their gear before setting out. The crew bosses and the strike team's complement of four rangers closed in around Lieutenant Garrett and waited.

"Does anybody want to admit they have the slowest crew?" the lieutenant asked them.

"If you're trying to figure out line order," Rodgers said, "my guys will take the far end. We're all military —" He paused there, and a shadow of some unpleasant thought drifted across his expression. "*Former* military, that is. The walk out to the end and the long walk back after hours will be easiest on us."

"Sounds good to me," Lieutenant Garrett said with a shrug. He pointed to one of the rangers, who nodded. "You're with Calvin Walker."

"Where do we start?" the ranger asked.

To answer, Lieutenant Garrett called up another map on his tablet. This one traced his proposed fire line but divided it into equal segments, or legs. The lieutenant focused the map on the first four legs of the fire line. He tapped the point at the head of the fourth leg. Its map coordinates and its GPS coordinates popped up next to it.

"Here," Garrett said. "Topography says it's on a hilltop but visibility won't be great until you start your line. Ready for coordinates?"

Sergeant Rodgers and the ranger each held up a hand. On his forearm, Rodgers wore a snug Nomex bracer that held a smartphone-sized tablet similar to the lieutenant's. Each of the Firestormers' crew bosses had one. The devices allowed Garrett to send them select information from his tablet, keeping everyone informed about the advance of the fire.

The rangers wore smart watches instead of the bracers. The watches connected wirelessly to high-tech glasses. Each pair of glasses included a tiny camera mounted next to the wearer's temple and a tiny speaker built into the earpiece. Next to the camera, a crystal-clear prism extended over the lens of the sunglasses, just outside the wearer's field of view. A microscopic, fiber-optic projector could display images into that prism, such as maps and weather data, for the rangers to review on site.

"Ready," Rodgers said, holding up his bracer. Walker, the ranger, nodded as well.

Lieutenant Garrett double clicked the coordinates he'd called up. He aimed his computer tablet in the two men's direction and swiped the image toward them. Rodgers' bracer and Walker's smart watch beeped.

"Got it," Walker said. Rodgers nodded.

"We'll take the anchor leg," Sergeant Rendon

said. "My crew is pretty quick. We'll keep the line bumping along."

"We'll take leg two." Richards said. To Rendon, he grinned and said, "Catch us if you can, Miss Molly." Rendon jokingly elbowed him in the ribs.

"That leaves you on leg three, Angel," Rendon said to Michael Raphael, the last crew boss. "Good luck ever getting a leg done."

"Less work for my team," Raphael said, feigning a careless shrug. "And don't call me Angel."

Lieutenant Garrett assigned a ranger to each crew and swiped them each a set of coordinates for where to begin. When they were all ready to go, he said, "Look, let's keep it careful and routine out there, okay?"

"We'll make sure you stay nice and bored," Sergeant Rendon said with a grin. "Just try not to fall asleep while we're out there doing all the hard work."

The crew bosses and their rangers laughed. Lieutenant Garrett laughed along with them. "No promises," he joked. "Now start walking."

One by one, the crew bosses saluted Lieutenant Garrett — first Rendon and then Richards and Raphael.

Sergeant Rodgers hesitated.

"Is there a problem?" Garrett asked him.

After a moment, Rodgers shook his head, forcefully saluted, and then turned and walked away into the forest.

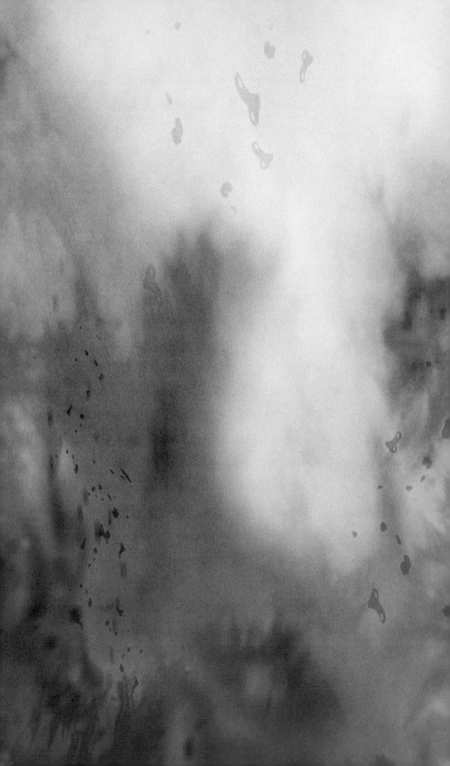

CHAPTER SIX

"That guy's a major problem," Sergeant Rodgers told Rendon as their crews hiked together toward the blaze.

They were still a half hour out from the fire lines Lieutenant Garrett had established, but the crews were already sluggish. The summer air hung hot and heavy in Klamath National Forest. Just breathing in the thick, smoky air was miserable, and the early morning sun had just peeked through the trees.

Not that the sun would be a concern. A blotchy black and gray smear stained the sky for miles in every direction, leaching light and color. On a better day, that gray overcast would have indicated an oncoming storm. But today, it signaled the opposite. The gray mass wasn't a cloud, but smoke, pouring upward from the ever-growing wildfire.

"What *guy* are you talking about?" Sergeant Rendon asked Rodgers. "The lieutenant?"

"If you want to call him that," Rodgers replied.

"You're not still bitter that MacElreath chose him instead of you?"

Rodgers scoffed. "It's hardly the first time I've been passed over for a promotion." *Although this time did sting the most*, he thought.

"Then what are you griping about?" Rendon pressed. "You really want to be stuck back at camp, handling paperwork and arguing with the chief? You're a grunt like me. You want to slash your way through this beast and help out the local departments like a hero. Am I right?"

Rendon reminded Rodgers of some of the women he'd served with in the military — tough, disciplined, and driven. He admired those things.

"Speaking of the local departments," Rendon began, "why did you really ask Garrett who the Hotshots were working those isolated fires?"

Sergeant Rodgers looked up at the sky. "Curiosity, I guess."

"Oh wow," Rendon replied, smirking. "We've really got to play poker sometime."

Rodgers grinned a little at that.

"Seriously, though," Sergeant Rendon said.

"The Lieutenant let it drop, but I know you better than he does."

"You both met me the same day in training," Rodgers pointed out.

"Sure, but you don't go out of your way to second-guess *me* in front of everybody, and you don't seem to think I don't belong here. If you did, I wouldn't pay you much attention either."

"Fair point," Rodgers muttered.

"So — and don't change the subject this time — what's up? Why the interest?"

Rodgers took a deep breath, considering not telling her. It wasn't her business any more than it was Garrett's. Still, he liked Rendon. He respected her. She was friendly and personable without letting it affect her professionalism. Plus, it wasn't like it was any big secret.

"I'm from here," he said, pulling the steel machete from his utility belt. "Not Klamath specifically, but not too far away. We used to come out here to hunt and fish and camp and that. My family and I did, that is."

"Do they still live out here?"

Sergeant Rodgers slashed at a few saplings in his path. "Here and there. They spread out a little when my parents retired."

"Are they military, like you?"

Rodgers shook his head. "I'm the only one who went in for that. The rest of them are all in the fire service. It wasn't until my last hitch ended that I joined the family business."

"Ah, I see," Sergeant Rendon said. "So you think some of them might be out here working this fire. Yeah?"

"Just one," Rodgers said. "My folks and my uncles are all retired out. My oldest brother's a fire marshal in San Diego, and the next one down works in Seattle. But my youngest brother, Ethan . . . he's a Hotshot with a company up north here. This fire's in their jurisdiction."

"Does Lieutenant Garrett know about this?"

"Doubt it. I never brought it up."

"It might be a good way to find out what you were asking about," Rendon pointed out.

"Doesn't matter," Sergeant Rodgers said. "I was just curious anyway. It's nothing worth bringing to Garrett's attention."

"Barring that," Rendon suggested, "you could always just call your brother. You know, if doing things the easy way doesn't gall you too much."

Rodgers shrugged uncomfortably and grunted.

Sergeant Rendon chuckled. "Slow down there,

Shakespeare. You want to put that in modern English for me?"

"It's not that big a deal," Rodgers said.

"So you're not going to call him or ask Garrett to find out if he's out here?"

"Nope."

"Why not?" asked Rendon.

Rodgers slashed at a few more saplings. "Ethan doesn't want to talk to me anyway."

"Why not?"

Rodgers sighed. "Because I don't feel like answering all of his personal questions whenever he starts prying into my business. Like you are."

Rendon huffed in frustration but didn't seem too offended by Rodgers' shutting her down. She elbowed him again and said, "You're no fun."

Rodgers gave her a faint grin. "Don't pout."

At that, Rodgers picked up his pace, allowing Rendon to fall behind him. Then he looked up at the gray sky again, and he thought about the last time he and his brother had spoken.

* * *

The problems began Thanksgiving of the previous year. The family had all piled into the home of Rodgers's eldest brother, Ian, to devour a fourteen-pound turkey and digest it over the course of several football games. The second game was just starting, but Rodgers had excused himself to the porch for a little peace and quiet. A big meal made him sleepy, but between his older brother William's kids, Ian's dogs, and the close quarters of Ian's living room, restful peace was in short supply.

Once outside, Rodgers plopped down in one of Ian's rocking chairs and stared out at the carpet of leaves that Ian called a front yard. Tufts of brown grass poked up through the leaves. Ian wasn't much for yard work.

Rodgers's peaceful meditation lasted all of five minutes.

"Well here's where you're hiding," Ethan said, letting the screen door bang behind him. He stomped onto the porch in his big steel-toe logging boots, zipping up a bomber jacket that used to belong to their father. He held a huge, Sherlock Holmes-style pipe. "Mind if I join you?"

"You're smoking now?" Rodgers asked him.

Ethan sat down on the porch rail and gestured toward Rodgers with the pipe. "Want to try it?"

"I'd rather live, thanks."

"Suit yourself," Ethan said with a shrug. "You don't know what you're missing." He took a deep breath in through his nose, stuck the stem of the pipe in his mouth, and blew through it. A steady stream of bright bubbles rose out of it and danced in the chilly November breeze.

Rodgers laughed despite himself. "You idiot."

Ethan smiled wider than the porch. "I got you. It's good to see you laughing again. You haven't done that much since you got back."

Rodgers shrugged.

"So how are you doing with . . ." Ethan gestured vaguely with the pipe, " . . . all that?"

"It's getting better," Rodgers said. "The guys at the VA hospital are helping out. Everything's pretty much okay."

"Good, good." Ethan paused, unsure what to add. "Glad to hear it. That's good."

Silence settled. Rodgers found it funny sometimes the way people tried to talk to him about his time in the military. No one seemed to know how to do it. At best, they talked around it. Most were only too happy to change the subject.

"So who are they watching for halftime in there?" he asked. The topic shift untied a knot of tension in his little brother's shoulders.

"Redskins, if you can believe it. As soon as halftime's over, they're going back to the Cowboys."

Ethan paused for a bit. He blew another stream of bubbles from his pipe, grinned at himself again, and then set the toy aside. Rodgers could tell he wanted to talk about something. Heath rocked back and closed his eyes, letting Ethan work his courage up.

"So, I've been reading about your program," he said at last.

"With the VA?"

"No, the Forest Service one. The Firestormers. I've been reading about you guys. You'll be doing good work. Mind if I ask you some questions about it?"

Heath shrugged but didn't open his eyes. "Sure."

"How'd you get involved? Did you . . . like . . . apply? Were you recruited? Is there some kind of list?"

Rodgers grinned to himself. "You wouldn't believe me if I told you."

"Come on, man."

"The former Secretary of State recommended me to the chief in charge of the program."

"What? Bull," said his brother.

Rodgers chuckled. "Why you asking, kiddo? You writing my biography or something?"

"No, I'm serious," Ethan insisted. "I want to know. I want to join."

Rodgers opened one eye to find his little brother staring at him. "For real?"

"Yeah, man. So do I have to apply, or . . . What?"

Rodgers sat forward in his chair and gave Ethan his best serious-older-brother stare — one the pair of them had seen plenty of times from Ian and William when they were kids.

"You don't want to do that," he said quietly.

"Why not? It can't be all that different from what I'm already doing."

"Exactly," Rodgers said. "You're a Hotshot, and doing a fine job at it. Being a Firestormer's just harder work for not much better pay."

"'A fine job'?" Ethan replied. "I'm actually a pretty great Hotshot, thank you. I just made crew boss last month. That's faster than you did it."

"So why are you in such a hurry to leave?"

"Because being a Firestormer's just . . . I don't know. Better. You guys are the elite. The elite *of* the elite. You said so yourself."

"It's not what it's cracked up to be."

"The heck it isn't," Ethan snapped. "You're

still in it. What's your problem with me wanting to be in it too? I'm not asking for a recommendation. I just want to know if I can fill out a dang application."

"I don't think it would suit you," Rodgers said, as nicely as possible, which wasn't very. "The on-call hours are a nightmare, and there's constant traveling during the fire season. Plus, right now there's no opportunity for promotion."

"Oh, this is such a load," Ethan barked, turning away once more. "Wouldn't suit me? What does that even mean? You don't think I can handle it?"

Rodgers paused to try to figure out how to phrase what he was thinking. The pause proved to be just a bit too long.

"You don't!" Ethan said when Rodgers didn't respond right away. "Oh, *that's* nice. You know, I've been a firefighter longer than you have, Heath. If you think you're so much better than me —"

"Boys," a voice called from behind the screen door. Rodgers and Ethan glanced over to see their mother standing inside, looking out at them. "Everything okay out here?"

"Yes, ma'am," they said together.

"The game's back on. Don't sit out here in the cold too long."

"Yes, ma'am," they said again.

Their mother nodded and shut the inner door. Rodgers and Ethan sat scowling in different directions a while longer. When no more words came from either of them, Ethan gave it up and pulled the screen door open.

"Wait, Ethan," Rodgers said, heaving a sigh. "There's an application process, and we are currently recruiting. Download the forms, get your lieutenant to sign them, and mail them to the address on our website. There's a written test, a couple of interviews, a background check, and a PT test. If you want to be a Firestormer, those are the hoops you've got to jump through. I can't do anything to help you out, though."

"I wouldn't expect you to," Ethan said. He looked down, a bitterly disappointed frown on his face. Then he went back inside in a huff.

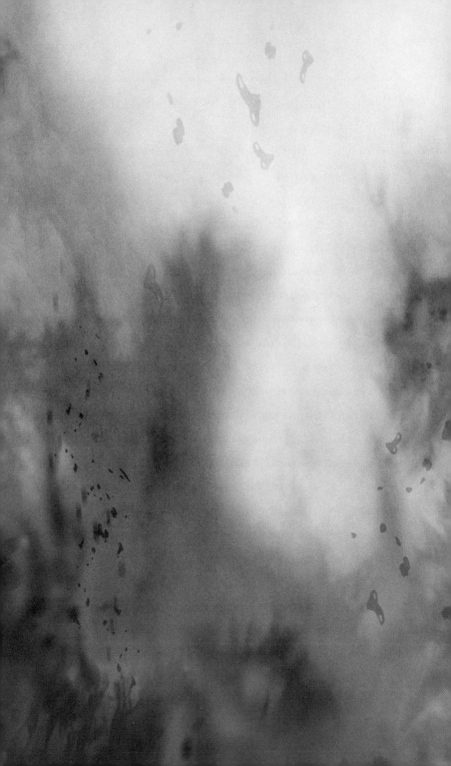

CHAPTER SEVEN

With a huff, Sergeant Amalia Rendon hoisted a roaring twenty-pound chain saw over her head.

"You saw like a girl!" a fellow Firestormer called out.

"Dang straight I do!" she hollered back, letting out a laugh

Behind her, a seventy-foot ponderosa pine slowly tipped and — *WHAM!* — came down with a thunderous crash.

Her four-person crew cheered.

Well begun is half done, Rendon thought. Of course, she knew that this fire was nowhere near half over.

As the felled pine settled on its side, Sergeant Rendon nodded to Corey Edwards, her crew's ranger, and said, "One down . . ."

" . . . and about a million to go," Edwards

responded. He grinned and gave her a quick salute and then headed off into the woods.

Sergeant Rendon nodded after him and set her shoulders. *Time to work.*

Less than an hour after splitting off from Rodgers and his crew, Rendon's crew had made significant progress on their fire line. It wasn't surprising, really. Amalia Rendon was one of the best and brightest among the elite of the elite.

For her, as with other Firestormers, fighting a wildland fire was relatively uncomplicated. Not easy, just uncomplicated. Sergeant Rendon and her crew scoured the terrain for natural firebreaks, such as canyons, rivers, stony fields or even highways. From those points, they cut fire lines through the wildland as tightly around the fire as possible. That meant taking down trees and slicing them into manageable logs with chain saws. That meant chopping down saplings and undergrowth with axes and breaking up the ground with picks.

It wasn't the sort of job one could like, exactly — it was too exhausting and nasty for that — but it afforded those who could handle it a unique and universal respect. Sergeant Rendon certainly appreciated that aspect of the work. That said, there were some days she wished saving the world didn't require quite so much backbreaking drudgery. And the work itself, while physically draining, did allow for a kind of meditative peacefulness once you got into the rhythm of it. The rhythm didn't make the work easier, but it made it easier to deal with.

Rendon sought that rhythm as the long, hard fight on the fire line began. She let her thoughts roll backward over the events that had brought her to where she was today. As her chain saw tucked into the fallen black ponderosa pine at her feet and the chips and dust flew, her mind worked its way back to the day she'd gotten the job. She thought she'd known what to expect then, but life had found a way — as it will — to surprise her.

* * *

Amalia Rendon hadn't had much occasion to head back into Albuquerque, New Mexico, since becoming a firefighter. As she fought traffic and searched for a parking space, she remembered why. Making her way from the car to the hotel where her interview was to take place, she was glad she'd decided against wearing the high heels that her previous job had required. She didn't think the occasion called for her beat-up old logging boots, but she also didn't want to skew too fancy either. Thus, her sensible Mary Janes.

Checking her watch, Rendon crossed the hotel lobby to the concierge desk to find out how to reach the business center. The young man behind the desk looked her up and down and then eagerly told her what she wanted to know. She politely declined his offer to physically walk her there himself.

Attached to the business center was a suite of offices. Chief Anna MacElreath had reserved one for the interview. According to the secretary who'd set up the appointment, MacElreath was traveling across much of the North- and Southwest to conduct the interviews because the government hadn't yet designated a headquarters for the program's staff. That, and she was also touring western hotspots to survey how local fire services conducted themselves on the job. A willingness to learn from the locals certainly seemed like a positive quality in a federal administrator. The fact that she'd also been the nation's first female smokejumper was another mark in her favor.

When she found the right room, Rendon straightened her interview jacket, brushed a sprig of lint off her pants leg, and knocked on the door.

"Come on in," a voice drawled from within. Rendon remembered when she heard it that MacElreath's online bio said she'd lived most of her life in Atlanta, Georgia.

Coming in, Rendon found the chief sitting behind a cheap desk with a dime-a-dozen pastoral landscape print hanging on the wall behind it. Chief MacElreath was taller than expected, and Rendon wondered if she had played college basketball like herself. The chief wore a long-sleeved, button-up shirt and khaki pants. A little less formal than Rendon's own outfit, but she was right not to have worn jeans and boots like she would've preferred.

"Welcome, Ms. Rendon," the chief said. "Nice suit."

Rendon smiled.

"Please, sit." Chief MacElreath shuffled some papers on her desk and then sat as well. "So I've been going over your work history, Amalia. Says here you started out doing weather for a local station after college."

Amalia cocked an eyebrow. "I think what it says is that I was the station's meteorologist. That was my major at UCLA. Well, one of them. That and journalism."

Chief MacElreath smiled at that. "Did you like it? Doing the weather on TV, I mean."

"It had its moments," Rendon replied. "It was just a job, though. Something to pay the bills."

"Says here you did some reporting as well."

"I did," Rendon said.

"Sounds like fun, being on TV. Why'd you want to give that up?"

"Well, I found something a little more worthwhile," Rendon said, trying not to let her irritation show. She'd expected at least one question relevant to her firefighting experience to have come up by now. Seeing as that wasn't the case, she decided to try to steer things back in the right direction herself.

"To be honest, I didn't like playing the 'weather girl' role the station wanted me to play, so I asked if I could put some field pieces together and do some real reporting. The station sent me out on a few fluff pieces as long as I promised to keep doing the weather."

"What sort of fluff pieces?" asked Chief MacElreath.

Rendon shook her head. "County fairs, store openings, movie shoots . . . That sort of thing. Nothing with substance. I complained for about a year, trying to get a story worth doing. Finally, they gave me something to shut me up. The station assigned me a series of stories with the Black Stand Hotshots out in Taos. I hung out with their crew for a couple of weeks, interviewing them, seeing how they train, and what they do on the job. I'd never even heard of Hotshotting before then. But by the time I was done, I realized they were doing a whole lot more good out there than I was ever going to do in front of a green screen."

"I'm glad to hear that you think that way," MacElreath observed. Rendon took a deep, calming breath rather than say the first thing that came to mind. "But, as far as that story you talked about goes, it didn't turn up in any of my research on you."

"Yeah." Rendon sighed. "After I finished, I gave it to my station manager, but he killed it without even looking at it. As soon as I got back to the station, he wanted me right back doing the weather 'where I belonged.' Apparently he didn't want me to actually enjoy that assignment. He was just trying to teach me a lesson. So we had us a little conversation about that. It ended with me spraining my wrist, bruising his jaw, and quitting my job all in one sentence."

MacElreath smothered a laugh. "That's when you joined the fire service, I gather," she went on. She checked her notes. "You didn't join up with the Black Stand crew, it looks like. Why not?"

"Couldn't get in, for one thing," Rendon said. "They had a full roster when I was interviewing them. I wouldn't have applied there anyway. I like the guys out there, and I respected what they were doing, but they treated me like I was their kid sister or their company mascot. Neither's a role I like to play."

MacElreath nodded, knowingly. "I see here you got on with a company up in Cloudcroft. Came in with a red card — that's impressive. Not too many women even want to be sawyers. How'd you learn to use a chain saw?"

"My mother," Rendon said, working hard to keep her tone flat, even, and professional. "She's a sculptor."

"Neat. Now, I spoke at some length with your captain out there. He speaks highly of your work. Says you've got a lock on a command of your own someday if you stay in Cloudcroft."

"That's kind of him," Rendon said. "I'd like to think I earned that."

"Tell me this, then, Amalia," pressed the chief, "if things are going so well, how come you want to leave?"

"You said you spoke to my captain, right? He told you about me?"

"That's right."

"What was the very *first* thing he told you about me?"

"He said you were pretty," MacElreath said.

"That's why I want to leave."

MacElreath frowned at that and nodded again. "Before we move on, I thought I'd let you know I'm hiring staff at the command level. I've got a public information officer position available if you're interested. With your news background, it might be something you're good at."

"I have no doubt I would be," Rendon said flatly. "That's not why I'm here, though. No offense to whoever you do find for that job, but I'd rather be out there in the field making a difference with a chain saw in my hands."

"Suit yourself." the chief said, shrugging. "Okay, last couple of questions . . . Are you married?'"

"Am I married?" Rendon shot back. "I'm not sure how that's relevant."

"It's not," said Chief MacElreath, smiling. "And I like that you told me as much."

"I don't follow," said Rendon, puzzled.

"Firefighting's not widely perceived as a woman's profession, even by many women. It's mostly done by men, and a lot of men — firefighters and otherwise — have some . . . unexpected opinions about women who want in. That question I asked you wasn't pass-fail. I just wanted to see how well you could keep your cool in the face of one of those opinions. Just in case you ever come up against somebody in the field who says that sort of stuff and means it."

"But I figured you out," Rendon said.

"True," MacElreath confirmed with a nod. "That tells me something just as important. Shows you don't lose your head in a stressful situation — a job interview, in this case — and not only think fast on your feet, but you're confident in who you are. That's the sort of attitude I like in my people."

Rendon was relieved. "But, Chief, I don't even think the good ol' boys ask those types of questions anymore."

"Not *anymore*," MacElreath said with a wink.

Rendon thought she knew exactly what that wink meant.

"And you're right, Rendon," the chief added. "Most of those 'good ol' boys' are learning. The young boys — the rookies — they hardly know any different. Heck, I trained half of those kids myself. And if you think for one moment, I'd tolerate —" Chief MacElreath stopped. "Well, I don't have to explain it to you."

Rendon gave a knowing nod.

"All I'm saying is that everyone on this crew deserves respect," the chief began again. "We treat each other as equals. And in a few years, we truly will be an equal team — fifty-fifty — at least if I have anything to say about it. And you, Rendon, are going to be a big part of that equation."

"Me?" Rendon pointed to herself. "Does that mean you want to offer me this job?"

"Was there any doubt?" MacElreath said, as if the conclusion were too obvious to put into words. "I had that decision made as soon as I saw your résumé and called your references."

"Oh," Rendon said. It felt like a chirp coming out of her mouth. "Um . . . You didn't want to just tell me that over the phone?"

MacElreath chuckled again. "To be honest, I would have if I'd just wanted you for a sawyer. But I've got a leadership position in mind for you, and for that I needed to put you through the wringer a little."

"Leadership?" Rendon asked, grinning. "I'd love to have my own strike team, if that's what you mean."

"I wish I could," MacElreath said. "Right now I've got the budget for exactly one elite strike team — and you're on it — but the leader's already been chosen by committee. What I can do, though, is make you a crew boss. For now. We can talk about more responsibility later, as our roster expands. Interested?"

Rendon didn't even have to think about it. "Absolutely. Although . . . let me ask you something."

"Go for it."

"What would've happened if I'd taken you up on that offer to be your public information officer?" Rendon questioned.

MacElreath blinked in surprise and laughed out loud. "Well, you would've made the person I already hired for that position very angry at you and me both. So I'm glad you didn't."

"So there was never another job?" Rendon asked, puzzled.

"There's only one place you should be," MacElreath said. "Welcome to the Firestormers."

CHAPTER EIGHT

"Welcome," began Chief MacElreath, staring out at a group of twenty reporters inside the Wilmond High School gymnasium.

The chief rubbed her eyes from overuse. She'd spent the past few hours reviewing plans and preparations and reading reports prepared by her staff. She'd also kept a close eye on the fire, checking its spread and making contingencies for one possible disaster scenario after another.

Chief MacElreath's staff hadn't taken a break either. Safety Officer Thomas White was glued to his computer, uploading fire, topography, and weather data into a program called Behave. With that information, Behave created models for how the fire would spread. Her liaison officer, David Holloway, communicated these models to every cooperating agency involved in the Klamath fire: the Forest Service, local firefighters, law enforcement, EMTs, aid agencies and the local community. Finally, Chief MacElreath's public information officer, Samantha Smalls, spent her morning fending off local and national media, whenever she could. When she couldn't, Smalls set up press conferences, like the one MacElreath was about to give.

"Earlier this week," Chief MacElreath continued, "multiple lightning strikes ignited fires in the Klamath National Forest. The first was here, in the area known as White Camp." She projected a map of the park on the screen behind her and highlighted the area. "The second was just south of Bear Pass. A third strike some hours later started another fire here." MacElreath highlighted the other areas and cropped the map to focus on them. She then tapped an icon, and the highlighted areas began to grow like a red stain spreading across the map.

"Local fire services dispatched to the scene kept the complex under observation at first," the chief continued, "but high winds and abundant fuel allowed the fires to spread toward one another more quickly than initially projected." As she spoke, the highlighted areas blended into one irregular, unified mass representing many hundreds of acres in area. It had taken the Forest Service the amount of time represented by that model to learn of the fire and contact MacElreath's Firestormers. "The Hillside and Wilmond residential communities were evacuated as a precaution. We haven't recorded any spread into the wildland-urban interface surrounding those communities, but the fire front is still too close for us to lift that evacuation order. We'll have more information on that as fire suppression efforts continue."

Chief MacElreath advanced the laptop to the next packet of data. This was a satellite photo of the entire burn area taken late the previous night. While its center was still a unified whole, questing tendrils of flame had begun to stretch out from that whole like the fingers of a hand. Some of those fingers were so vast that other smaller fingers spread off from them.

"Last night and this morning, we managed to put together a complete map of the affected area," she said. "This was taken around midnight. And this is our best estimate of the fire's growth pattern over the next twenty-four hours."

Chief MacElreath overlaid a second projection

on that image and animated it. The animation extended the larger and smaller fingers of flame farther across the forest, showing where the wildfire was most likely to spread. The two largest fingers stretched dangerously close to the evacuated area. A third, smaller finger pointed in the direction of the Wilmond community.

As the animation played, MacElreath took a moment to look up at the room. Most of the attendees were news crews from a couple of competing stations. A few more were state and national reporters — most of whom the chief recognized from previous fires in California.

"Any questions so far?" the chief asked the crowd. A few hands went up, and MacElreath pointed to a familiar face in the front row.

"What's burning, Chief?" the reporter asked.

"The usual suspects, Terry," she told him. "Timber, litter, understory. It's thick, so it's burning fast. It blew up a lot faster than any of the local fire services could react to them, much less contain them. That's why the Forest Service called us in."

"Speaking of the local fire service," the reporter asked, "we were told yesterday that the incident commander at this complex was Captain Pete

Kinsey. Can you shed some light on why he was removed from command?"

Chief MacElreath put on her best poker face. "Captain Kinsey wasn't removed; he stepped down. He's still taking part in suppression efforts under the direction of Operations Section Chief Michael Farrant. His crews have been deployed here." The Chief highlighted an area south of the fire closest to Wilmond. "He's overseeing containment of this finger of the fire. Captain Kinsey's firefighters are the ones standing directly between that fire and this command post."

MacElreath paused a moment to let the reporters make of that what they would. Despite her distaste for Kinsey's personality, she and Holloway had done the captain a favor. If Kinsey was as upwardly mobile as the young man thought he was, MacElreath might have to call on that gratitude in the field someday when Kinsey was in command of more resources.

"All right," she said in conclusion, "that's my spiel. We can talk about specific resource numbers if you like, but Miss Smalls here has already compiled all that information on InciWeb and northern California's own coordination center website." The chief advanced the presentation to its last slide, which listed the information websites.

"Any final questions?" Chief MacElreath asked.

Nobody raised their hands — except for one guy sitting by himself in the farthest back corner of the room. He wasn't wearing any press credentials, which meant he was probably an Internet reporter whom Smalls had deemed legit enough to let into the briefing. The man stood. He didn't look too much older than the students would who filled this gymnasium under normal circumstances.

"Ms. MacElreath, I have a question," the kid said. "Can we see the overhead shot of the fire again?"

"Sure," said Chief MacElreath, putting it back up on the board. "What's your name?"

"Topher Smith," he said. "I'm the president of the Lost and Forgotten Foundation."

"LAFF?" MacElreath asked with a slight grin. Some of the reporters chuckled obligingly.

Smith's face reddened a little and he frowned defensively. "I'm an independent reporter covering environmental stories. I'm also a vlogger. My YouTube channel's got over fifty-thousand subscribers."

Samantha Smalls leaned into the chief and said quietly in her ear, "He's small time, but he's legit. He does a lot of local coverage. Pretend like you just recognized him. It'll make his day."

"Right," Chief MacElreath said to Smith, nodding as Smalls stepped back. "Sorry I didn't recognize you. I must be more familiar with your work than your face." She offered Smith a smile. "What's your question?"

"I'm wondering what your plans are to put out that tendril there on the left," the vlogger asked, pointing vaguely at the screen.

Chief MacElreath highlighted the smaller of the two fingers. "This one?"

"No, below that, and to the left. Where that first lightning strike started."

MacElreath looked at her laptop screen and highlighted the area Smith was referring to. As fingers went, this was the least developed. Thus far, unfavorable wind and a relatively low density of fuel had slowed its spread to a crawl. The Behave models didn't foresee it making much progress in the next twenty-four to forty-eight hours.

"It's not a priority," Chief MacElreath told him. "Is there —"

"Are you aware," Smith cut in, "that the area just to the west of that tendril is one of the last suitable habitats of northern California's Humboldt marten?"

Chief MacElreath cocked an eyebrow. "What's that — a bird?"

"Not that kind of martin," Smith said, with an exasperation that indicated he'd made that correction often. "The marten — with an E — is a fur-bearing omnivore that lives in the forest. The Humboldt marten, specifically, is almost extinct. There's only about one hundred of them left in all of California, what with logging and wildfires and human expansion and —"

"And they live in this area of the forest?" the chief asked, cutting Smith off before he could build up a head of steam.

"Yes, ma'am. They've been spotted there."

"And they're endangered?" Chief MacElreath asked. She usually got reports from the Forest Service when an area in the path of a wildfire was a protected habitat of an endangered species. This was the first she'd heard about any sort of marten-with-an-E.

"Well, not exactly," Smith said. "They're not specifically on the list, but we're working on it. I personally signed a petition to get them protected under the Endangered Species Act. Your own agency said they ought to be protected, but then dragged its feet when it came time to make its listing decision. You missed your deadline to do the right thing. Now you want a ten-year study to see if protection is warranted."

Smith was building steam again, and other reporters were starting to take notes. Chief MacElreath clenched and unclenched her jaw.

"Dealing with the endangered species list is outside my span of control," she said. "I can't speak to it. It also happens not to be relevant to this incident."

"Not relevant?" Smith barked. "I just told you the martens' sanctuary is in the way of your fire. All I'm asking is what you're doing about it."

"This finger of the fire is not a priority at this time," the chief said, trying not to say it through clenched teeth. "It's not spreading with any due speed — certainly not as fast as these others. This area is included in the containment plan, but we have to attack the more aggressive and fast-moving fire fronts first."

"But what about the martens?"

"Frankly, I've got bigger fish to fry at the

moment. Now, if we don't have any more questions, I need to get back to work."

Before anyone else could say anything, Chief MacElreath stepped away from the podium, gave the floor to Smalls, and left. She didn't look at Smith again, but she could feel the young man's angry, disappointed eyes on her all the way out.

* * *

"Bigger fish to fry?" Smalls said later in MacElreath's office. "You know you're a fire chief, right? Could you have thought of a more sensitive way to say that?"

"I considered it," MacElreath said. Smalls wasn't quite as annoyed as she sounded, but the chief knew that she'd just made Smalls's day ten times harder. "You talked him down, I assume."

"Oh sure," she replied. "But it took me half an hour of my day I'm never getting back."

"All right then. Did he go home at least?"

"Oh no. He's been hammering away on his laptop all morning, rallying his subscribers. But you want to know the worst thing?"

"Not really."

"After you left, a couple of the new guys started asking him questions — Smith. They wanted to know about these weasels he's so on about. I steered the briefing back off the rocks as best I could, but when it was over, half of them left the room with their heads together."

"You think this is a problem?"

"Not yet," Smalls said, "but it could be. These local guys report on wildfires all the time, and it's always pretty much the same. If this marten business spices the story up for them and it looks like we don't care . . . Yeah, that's a problem."

"Well then, I have the perfect solution," Chief MacElreath said. "I'll let my talented public information officer stop the bleeding." MacElreath smiled, mostly because she knew that Smalls could handle it. Smalls did remind the chief of her younger self, after all. "Meanwhile, I'm going to put out an eleven-thousand-acre fire before people start losing their homes. Sound good?"

Smalls took a long, deep breath, and then nodded respectfully.

"Sometimes, we all have to play the hand we're dealt, Smalls," offered the chief before burying her face in her laptop again, checking in on Lieutenant Garrett's progress.

CHAPTER NINE

Back at the Klamath camp, Lieutenant Garrett buried his face in his laptop again. His responsibilities as strike team leader gave him no opportunities to fall asleep, much less get bored. Although he wasn't on the fire line himself, digging firebreaks, it was his responsibility to monitor the progress of his crew and communicate that progress to Incident Command. To that end, he had a few tools at his disposal — some of which he'd never dreamed of needing while working structure fires in the burbs.

The main communication tool was his radio. With a flick of a button, he could switch between three frequencies on which he carried out three different conversations. The main frequency was his channel back to Incident Command. From them, he got big-picture information about the overall spread of the fire, weather conditions, and the availability of supplies and air support. The second channel connected him to his crew bosses. If they were straying too far from his fire line, he could correct their courses. If they were falling behind schedule, he could urge them to pick up the pace. The third channel connected Garrett to his rangers. These Firestormers didn't carry hand tools or chain saws. Instead, they carried binoculars, ropes, tree-climbing spurs, maps, and a five-gallon bladder bag of water with a hand-pump sprayer. It was each ranger's job to orbit their crew, scouting the area for dangers. They also developed escape routes should the fire advance faster than they could contain it.

The two-way radio was the lowest-tech part of Garrett's equipment. His tablet was more powerful than his personal computer. It was wrapped in a waterproof, shock-resistant casing. He could drop it down a rocky hill and expect to find it perfectly functional at the bottom. The tablet was the heart of Garrett's capabilities in the field, as well as his lifeline back to Incident Command in an emergency. Without it, he'd be blind to ongoing fire and weather conditions. He'd have to rely on hand drawing lines on paper maps as his crews and rangers reported their status. It could be done — it *had been* done for decades — but the tablet made everything so much easier.

Yet, despite the sci-fi level technology, everything came down to the sweat and toil of Firestormers on the front lines. Lieutenant Garrett could direct their efforts and watch over them remotely, but it was up to them to get the job done. And if there was anything his brief, intensive field training had taught him, it was that that job *sucked*.

Lieutenant Garrett knew the basic strategy of fighting a wildfire was simple enough. Map out the total area of the fire. Then surrounded it with non-flammable firebreaks, so the blaze couldn't grow any larger. When the area was accessible by roads, bulldozers could cut those firebreaks. In this case, however, that wasn't an option. That left the work to Firestormers, who set to it with strength and obsessive determination. Their job was to clear lines that were miles long and dozens of feet wide of everything from trees to brush to grass. They'd clear-cut the area and dig it down to the soil, so that nothing left would burn.

Each five-person crew boasted two sawyers, armed with gasoline-powered chain saws. They were responsible for bringing down trees along the fire line and cutting them into manageable chunks. Moving behind them was the swamper, whose job it was to drag those chunks off the fire line. The swamper also carried the extra gas, oil, and tools to keep the sawyers' saws working.

The rest of the crew followed with hand tools doing the hottest, nastiest, dirtiest work. With hard, sharp shovels, Pulaski fire axes, and steel fire rakes, they uprooted undergrowth and broke up the underlying dirt until nothing remained. They called themselves grunts, because by the end of a backbreaking shift, they were barely capable of speaking more than that.

At camp, Garrett sweltered in the California heat, and he didn't have a hundred-foot wall of fire to contend with. He could hear the roar of the distant blaze, and it set his instincts on edge. He felt guilty. Garrett knew he was capable of doing the work his crews were doing — he wouldn't have made it into the Firestormer program otherwise — but he preferred the demands that being in charge thrust on him instead.

As the day went on, Lieutenant Garrett couldn't help wonder if that preference meant he wasn't truly Firestormers material. If he'd made it onto the team as a grunt rather than riding his father's influence to the rank of lieutenant, could he hack it on the line? Could he do the work and keep up good spirits the way Rendon seemed able to do? Could he attack the problem with endless gung-ho determination like Rodgers? He didn't know, and not knowing bothered him.

If he was asking these men and women to follow his lead, they needed to feel like he was one of them. They needed to know they could count on him. They needed to know they could trust him, as they trusted one another.

Just then, Lieutenant Garrett received an incoming call on this two-way radio. "Go ahead, Chief?" He prompted MacElreath, awaiting her hourly updates from Incident Command.

"Yep . . . Got it . . . Yep . . . The bird? . . . Oh . . . Really?" Garrett listened and responded as the chief rattled off a list of questions and updates. "Rodgers? Yes, ma'am, he's on the fire line with his crew . . . Oh . . . Okay . . . Yep, I'll make sure he gets the message."

Lieutenant Garrett switched off the radio. *The first day on a big fire is always the worst*, he thought.

CHAPTER TEN

Sergeant Rodgers loved the first day on a big fire. He reveled in it. His bull-necked, all-veteran crew was at the head of today's fire line. That meant they constantly bumped into uncut territory and hiked through the toughest forests.

Rodgers was an old-hand at orienteering, and he had personal experience with these woods. Still, in an area the size of Klamath National Forest, he would've been hopelessly lost without his lifeline back to Lieutenant Garrett and without his intrepid ranger, Calvin Walker.

His lifeline was the tough smartphone-sized datapad secured in the Nomex bracer on the inside of his right forearm. On it, he checked maps and satellite imagery of the area in real time, and Lieutenant Garrett sent him information from up the Incident Command pipeline. The datapad also tracked him via GPS and kept Garrett informed of his location.

As invaluable as the datapads were, Rodgers actually found himself relying on his ranger more. Calvin Walker helped Rodgers's crew stay on course through the trackless forest or guide them around obstacles that would have cost them countless time backtracking.

Walker didn't stick around to chitchat when he checked in periodically — he didn't even eat his lunch with the crew. So it was surprising that he was nearby when Garrett checked in at midday.

Rodgers pressed the Accept button on the datapad. "Afternoon, Lieutenant. What's the matter . . . don't trust us to do our job out here?"

Rodgers smiled at Walker, and Walker smiled back hesitantly.

Lieutenant Garrett hemmed and hawed on the other end of the line.

"Get on with it, sir," Rodgers blurted out. "Some of us have work to do."

"There's a problem," Garrett admitted.

"Is something going on?" Rodgers asked, recognizing the seriousness in his voice.

"That team that was working the isolated fire to the south —remember them?" Garrett asked.

Yeah, of course I do, Rodgers thought.

"The Hotshots? They're missing."

"How the heck did that happen?"

"It started with radio trouble last night," Garrett explained. "They were breaking up all through the end of the day. Patchy signal. Garbled transmissions. Operations Section said they made an almost unintelligible transmission at the end of their shift when they were returning to base. They should have checked in this morning, but they haven't yet. They're completely silent, and their fire's starting to slip containment."

"That's a problem," Rodgers said. If the lower fire burned up to the main mass, it was going to catch the Firestormers from behind and Incident Command would have to redraw new containment lines around the whole area.

"That isn't all," Garrett said.

Rodgers's blood ran cold. His fingers numbed.

"Those Hotshots . . ." the lieutenant continued. "They're the Okanogan Badgers."

"That's my brother's company."

"I know," Lieutenant Garrett said. "Sergeant Rendon radioed me this morning and told me you had a brother working out here."

Of course she did, Rodgers thought.

"I just spoke with Chief MacElreath at Incident Command," continued the lieutenant. "She confirmed that the crew is missing."

"Well, what's being done?" Rodgers demanded. "Is search and rescue out yet?"

"They've got a helicopter coming."

Rodgers shook his head. "Over those woods, a helicopter's not going to be much help. They need people on the ground, searching the area. People who know the land."

"I know," Garrett said. "That's the plan. The helicopter's just a Band-Aid."

"And I need to be with them," Rodgers said, not listening to Garrett. "I know this area pretty well, and I've done search and rescue before."

"I know," Garrett said.

"Look, he's my brother, Lieutenant," Rodgers said, his volume rising. "I'm doing this. I'll start walking from here if I have to."

"Whoa, take it easy, Heath," Garrett said. "I agree with you. In fact, search and rescue's coming to pick you up right now. That's what the helicopter's for. They're going to take you and Walker over to your brother's camp to start looking. In the meantime, I've split the rest of your crew up between Rendon and Richards."

Rodgers blinked a few times, too dumbstruck to react. He looked down at the thermos in his hand. Finally he said, "You already did all that?"

"As soon as they told me about your brother," Garrett replied. "I just assumed you'd want to go help find him. That's what I would want to do."

"Thanks."

Lieutenant Garrett grunted. "Sure. Helicopter should be there in five minutes. Get what you need, and be ready to go."

"Will do," Walker chimed in for both of them.

Rodgers heard the lieutenant switch off his radio, and he did the same. Then he turned to Walker. "Ethan," Rodgers said quietly. "His name's Ethan. My baby brother."

Walker squeezed Rodgers's shoulder. "We'll find him."

"He'd be here right now if it weren't for me."

* * *

A couple of weeks before fire season officially started, Chief MacElreath had called Rodgers into her office at the Firestormers' headquarters. Rodgers's first suspicion, irrational though it may have been, was that Lieutenant Garrett had already written him up for something stupid, and he was being called on the carpet for it. He took a seat across the oak desk from the chief and mentally prepared himself to deal with a hassle.

"Good lord, C-3PO, why don't you try to relax?" Chief MacElreath said, grinning. "I've never seen anybody try to be at attention sitting down before. Take it easy. This isn't the principal's office."

Rodgers grinned despite himself and relaxed in his chair. Though he wasn't a fan of the chief's sense of humor, it had a certain charm. Her south Georgia accent lent it a disarming folksiness.

"So what can I do for you, Chief?"

"PT tests were yesterday for the potential recruits," Chief MacElreath said. "I'm having everybody who passed sit down with Garrett for some one-on-one interviews. After that, you and the other crew bosses can go over their files and cherry-pick which ones you want. Final say is up to Garrett, but I trust you four to work out any disagreements before you take your picks to him."

"I doubt that'll be a problem," Rodgers said. "We know what we like in our crews."

"Good, good. Now, before any of that stuff happens, there was a matter I wanted to bring up with you personally first. You know your brother Ethan put in his application this round, yes?"

Rodgers nodded. His mom had mentioned it the last time he'd talked to her. Ethan hadn't had much to say to him since Thanksgiving.

"I had a good long chat with him during our interview," said the chief. "Seems like a good kid."

"He didn't bring up my name, did he?"

MacElreath shook her head. "I practically had to drag it out of him that you're his brother. You aren't even listed on his application. He's pretty concerned about the appearance of favoritism. He told me he didn't want any special consideration."

"That's good," Rodgers said, secretly relieved.

"Frankly, though, he kind of needs it," Chief MacElreath went on. "Your brother's a good firefighter and all, don't get me wrong. There's not so much as a write-up for showing up late to work in his file. But for all there's nothing negative, there's nothing outstanding in there either. He just gets the job done, and that's pretty much it. The captains he's worked for were polite about it when I called them, but they all agree."

Rodgers frowned, unsure what the chief wanted from him. "How'd he do on the tests?"

Chief MacElreath glanced at her computer monitor. "Not bad. Solid B on the written. Passed the practical, but you've pretty much got to cut your own foot off to fail that part. He was borderline on the PT test. Did okay on the pack run, but his time was on the bad side of the curve.

Rodgers winced. "I'm not sure what I can say to that, Chief."

"Just tell me this," Chief MacElreath said. "The reason I called you in here is because I don't know your brother like you know him. He's pretty young. In my eyes, he's borderline, but he might have potential. You know him. Does he have what it takes — right now — to be one of us, or should I send him back to the minors to train up for a season?"

"Send him back," Rodgers shot back.

"You don't want to think about that a little?"

Rodgers shook his head. "I don't think he's ready."

"He's been fighting fires longer than you have," MacElreath pointed out.

"It wasn't just my firefighting experience that got me here," Rodgers said. "Ethan's never really sought out challenges. That's why he hasn't distinguished himself yet. Turning him down might help put that in perspective for him."

"It could light a fire under him, I suppose," Chief MacElreath said. She thought about it a moment, scratching idly at her wrist under the cuff of her sleeve. "All right, then. I'll cut him and have a chat with him about it."

"Sounds good," Rodgers said. "Is there anything else?"

"I appreciate your candor. I don't want you to go away feeling like you threw your brother under the bus. I needed your honest opinion."

"It's for his own good," Rodgers replied. "And the good of the team, of course."

"True, true."

Rodgers rose, said his goodbyes, and headed for the door. Before he could leave, Chief MacElreath called him back one last time.

"Hey, Heath? Your brother can always apply again next year. I'll make that clear to him."

"Yes, ma'am."

"And this program's always growing," Chief MacElreath added. "This time next year, if he makes the cut, you might just have a strike team of your own to put him on."

"Yes, ma'am," Heath said again. "Definitely something worth thinking about."

CHAPTER ELEVEN

Sergeant Rendon sat on a sawn log, thinking. As she did, she sharpened up the teeth of her chain saw with a long file. The old beast had been chewing up trees all day, and it was starting to go a little dull on her.

The file's back-and-forth metallic scraping made a raspy sort of music that made Rendon grin and think of her mother sitting on a stump back home doing the same thing.

"We're all cleaned up," her second sawyer, Alex, told her as he came ambling over. The cargo pockets of his fire-resistant Nomex pants bulged with the plastic wrapping from the MRE he'd eaten. His chain saw hung propped casually on one shoulder. "Are we pushing on or waiting for Raphael's crew to bump us?"

"We'll give them 'til I finish with this," Rendon

replied, gesturing with her file. "Or until our ranger checks in — whichever comes first."

"Got it." Alex ambled away again to relay the news to the others.

Like the other Firestormers, Sergeant Rendon's crew was working in a bump-and-jump pattern designed to eat up miles of fire and keep the work moving smoothly. Their strike team leader back at camp — Lieutenant Garrett — had established the prospective fire line on an interactive map on his laptop and divided it up into equal segments. Sergeant Rendon's crew was slightly faster on average than the other three crews, leaving long gaps in the fire line between themselves and the other crews. Rendon hoped that Sergeant Rodgers's crew and the others could pick up the pace because gaps in the fire line weren't ideal. But Rodgers had been surprisingly absent from communication over the past couple of hours.

Those gaps would have been fairly dangerous if not for the rangers attached to each of the crews. Unlike the sawyers and swampers working on the line, Corey Edwards and the other three rangers swept out around their crews on their own, keeping an eye on things at a safe distance.

Moving inside and outside the unfinished fire line, they monitored the progress of the fire and made constant reports on the evolving conditions. They also stayed in contact with their crew bosses, making sure the line was proceeding on course, or helping redirect it around unforeseen obstacles.

The rangers even occasionally helped direct air tankers and helicopters deployed by the Air Operations branch back at the Incident Command Post, acting like Air Force combat controllers on the ground in enemy territory. While Sergeant Rendon and her crew kept their heads down and focused on the work in front of them, Edwards and the other rangers kept them safe against the unpredictable whims of the ravenous wildfire.

A couple of minutes of filing later, Edwards's call came in on the radio.

Sergeant Rendon checked his GPS position on her datapad. That datapad was her lifeline out to Edwards and to Lieutenant Garrett at camp. It also held her maps of the area and kept her updated on the schedule of Air Operations' air tanker flyovers.

Early in her career, her first Hotshot crew had been caught unaware when an air tanker had buzzed over her line raining fire-retardant foam on the area. None of the heavy chunks had hit anyone, luckily, but spatter from the bombardment had dyed all their clothes and gear and exposed skin sickly pink for the rest of the job. Rendon had no intention of letting that ever happen again.

"Go ahead, Edwards," Sergeant Rendon said.

"Hey, Sergeant," the ranger replied. "We've, um . . . I think we have a problem."

Sergeant Rendon set her chain saw aside and stood up, her blood running cold. Edwards's GPS marker on the map showed he was about half a mile out ahead of the finished part of the line and just outside it. "What is it?"

"It's not an emergency, exactly. I mean, not for us, I guess. Well, maybe. I don't think there's even a code for it."

Sergeant Rendon frowned. Edwards didn't sound rattled or even particularly alarmed. He sounded . . . confused.

"What's going on?" she asked him.

"Well, there's . . . there's *people* out here," Edwards told her. "Right in the middle of where the next leg has to go through."

"What?" Rendon gasped. "You're kidding me, right? The area has been evacuated."

"I wish I was kidding," Edwards said. "Can you come ahead and meet me? They want to talk to somebody in charge."

"Oh crap. Yeah, I'll be right there."

CHAPTER TWELVE

"Oh crap," muttered Rodgers, looking out of the window of the search-and-rescue chopper.

On the ground below, he saw that the isolated fire his brother was working was in danger of growing out of control. Already, the lower fire had begun to spread out from containment. Tendrils of flame spread out through the opening like a hand desperately clawing up out of a well. If the contained part of the fire were a seed, these tendrils were the shoots pushing out for sun and air. As they spread, a high wind rose in the south, whipping the flames up higher and pushing them out farther and faster. Time was running out to get this fire back under control.

All hope was not lost, however. Now that search and rescue was involved, it was just a matter of time before Sergeant Rodgers and the searchers found Ethan and his crew. If everyone was all right, Rodgers could reconnect them with Incident Command and get them back to work. In the meantime, the suppression effort still had one thing going for it: the Air Operations branch.

On a fire of this size, air operations were essential. In the early stages, light planes such as the Firestormers' CASA-212 delivered smokejumpers to remote regions of the fire. As the suppression effort developed, smaller cargo planes delivered supplies to those crews camping near the fire lines. Search-and-rescue operations and medical evacuation missions were handled by helicopter. More recently, tech specialists from the Incident Command staff had begun to employ quad-rotor and fixed-wing UAV drones to monitor fire conditions and keep up with suppression efforts.

Even more important was the role Air Operations played in the direct suppression effort. On fires like this one, a fleet of air tankers ran continuous missions over the burning land, carrying one thousand to twenty thousand gallons of fire retardants. When they were over the right area, they opened their tanks and spread their payloads like bombers dropping explosives.

Water was the preferred payload, as choppers could pump it into their tanks via hose from local sources or dunk and fill collapsible "Bambi buckets" suspended underneath. Some planes could even skim water right off the surface of a large enough body and drop payload after payload wherever they were needed.

Certain chemical retardants were in common use as well, especially early in the suppression effort. Combining select phosphates with thickeners, preservatives and other additives, the chemicals blanketed a target area with sticky, lumpy clumps that cut off the fire's oxygen and suffocated it. As the chemicals broke down, they acted as fertilizers to help the burnt land recover.

The planes and choppers that made up the Air Operations fleet were the property of the Forest Service for wildfire suppression. Their activities were coordinated from Incident Command, under the umbrella of Operations Section. In sweeping coordinated flights, the tankers either swarmed isolated fires or flew along the fire lines to supplement ground efforts.

Sergeant Rodgers was normally too busy to even think about ongoing air operations, but today he had a good perspective on the entire aerial mission. For as far as the eye could see, Forest Service tankers and helicopters dipped in and out of the smoke and over the flames like a swarm of bees. Thinking about the organization that kept them all out of each other's way made his job of hiking long miles and digging ditches seem like child's play.

I'll leave that headache to Garrett, he thought.

An alert on Rodgers's datapad beeped, drawing his attention back toward the ground. Walker's smart watch beeped at the same time.

"This is the place," Walker said, checking his watch against the readout on the projector lens built onto his smart goggles. "I think."

They had arrived at the site where Operations Section Chief Michael Farrant said Ethan and company had built their camp. Rodgers wore a frown to match the uncertainty in Walker's voice. He tapped the helicopter pilot on the shoulder and signaled him to take a lap around the area. The pilot nodded and banked the aircraft into a long, slow turn.

"It's burned," Rodgers said. Below them, the ground was black and smoldering with gnarly skeletal fingers of burnt tree trunks sticking out irregularly. *A complete boneyard,* Rodgers thought.

Some two hundred yards away lay the break in the Okanogan Badgers' fire line. A strategic air tanker bombardment had temporarily doused the fire on this spot, but there was no sign left of any campsite.

"This is awfully close to the fire line," Walker observed. "Bad place to set up."

"Do you —" Rodgers began. His voice caught in his throat, and he had to start again. "Do you see any bodies?"

"No."

"Okay . . . So if they were here, that means they got out."

Walker nodded thoughtfully. "So where do you reckon they'd go? Back to their buggy?"

"They should. Do we know where it is?"

Walker tapped his smart watch to life and began flicking through apps on the touchscreen. He kept his eye on the projection screen in his goggles until he had the information he wanted. When he got it, he swiped the information he'd found from his smart watch toward Rodgers's datapad. Rodgers looked out the window vaguely in the direction of where the buggy should have been parked, but smoke made it impossible to see.

"This is where they should be going," Rodgers

said to the pilot, holding up the datapad beside him. The pilot glanced at the map depicted on the small screen and pointed the helicopter in the right direction. The fire wasn't spreading that way yet, but it was only a matter of time.

As the helicopter drew closer, Walker finally spotted the Badgers' buggy parked at a scenic overlook with an old set of stairs leading down to an overgrown hiking trail. The aircraft's rotors tore the low-hanging smoke over the area to shreds as it descended to give the spotters a clearer view.

"I hope this isn't his escape route," Sergeant Rodgers said. "It's all uphill and overgrown. What are you thinking, Ethan?"

Walker said nothing, but Rodgers could see the ranger shared his opinion. Escaping uphill from any danger was always a bad call. Trying to escape from a fire uphill was even worse. Wildfire traveled faster uphill.

"See anything?" the pilot called over his shoulder.

"There's nobody here," Rodgers said. "They must still be out in the woods."

"Maybe they're trying to dig new lines around the fire where it got out," Walker suggested.

"Without calling it in?" Rodgers asked. "And

with their camp torched? No. Ethan knows better than that. He's trying to get his people back here. At least he'd better be . . ." He turned to the pilot. "Take us back over the canopy. We'll try to spot their trail in the middle somewhere."

"Heath . . ." Walker began.

"It's all right," Rodgers cut him off. "I remember this area pretty well from when I was a kid. I know some places we can start looking to try to pick them up."

"Does your brother know the area as well as you do?"

Rodgers frowned. He held out a hand and tipped it side to side. "So-so. He didn't come out here as often." Walker's dubious expression did not fade. "It's all right, I've got an idea." He turned back to the pilot and laid that idea out. The pilot shrugged and guided the helicopter back the way they'd come.

The last leg of the flight was short, but it felt like an eternity to Rodgers. *Come on, Ethan*, he thought. *Where are you?*

CHAPTER THIRTEEN

"Where are they?" Sergeant Rendon asked her ranger, who was sitting on a rock, looking glum. She did not see anyone else.

"Okay, Edwards," she said through a wry grin, "if this is some weird ploy to get me alone in the woods, you've got some explaining to do."

The ranger looked up and flushed bright red. Two distinct shades of embarrassment shone in his eyes. His words stumbled over each other for almost thirty seconds as he hastily tried to explain that that was definitely not the case.

"Relax," Rendon told him. "I'm just teasing. Where are these people who shouldn't be here?"

Looking somehow relieved and further embarrassed at the same time, Edwards jumped down from his rock and motioned her forward. "This way."

Sergeant Rendon set off after him through a dense cluster of ponderosa pine on a winding path. It looked just like every other random space between any two given trees.

"So how many people are we dealing with out here?" she asked.

"Not sure," Ranger Edwards said. "They didn't too much like me showing up unannounced. Didn't feel much like showing me around. They agreed to talk to my boss, but they wouldn't let me wait down here with them. It's probably just as well I came back, though. I don't know if you'd have been able to find the place on your own."

"I'd have you on GPS," Sergeant Rendon pointed out, gesturing with the datapad on her forearm.

"That wouldn't help much in woods like this," Ranger Edwards said, patting a tree trunk as he went by it. "Heck, if I hadn't tramped this trail down so much on my way out, I would've had a hard time finding the way back myself."

Rendon shook her head. If this nontrail was what Edwards considered easy to follow, she'd hate to have seen a difficult one.

In another few minutes of winding their way through the woods, the two of them reached their destination. The trail emptied out into a long-ago dried out streambed that split in the middle around a jagged upthrust of stones. Beyond the stones, built onto the side of a thickly wooded hill, was the start of a tiny little village of spruce-log cabins. Wisps of smoke rose up from narrow stone chimneys and wildflowers grew up through the space beneath the hide-curtained windows. There were no roads, no vehicles, and no animals larger than dogs. What few dogs they could see all either immediately started barking or ran and hid in the shadows of the trees all around.

"How exactly did you find this place?" Sergeant Rendon murmured with a sidelong glance at Edwards.

"I saw the chimney smoke," he said just as quietly. "I thought a spot fire had started, so I came down here to put it out. Then I met them."

"Them" referred to the twenty or so people Edwards could see standing in front of their houses looking at the two newcomers as if they were visitors from another world. In a way, perhaps they were.

Among the crowd was a fairly even mix of men and women and another half of the total in children. The children's faces showed a mingling of fear and curiosity, tipping toward the latter the younger the kids were. The women were all stony-eyed and quiet. The men glared with suspicion. A knot of them stood by the stones that marked the entrance to the tiny village, quietly conferring with one another. Five of them broke away from the main group and came forward as Rendon and Edwards approached.

"Well what's this now?" the one in the center said, gesturing at Rendon but looking at Edwards.

This one, the apparent leader, was older than Edwards by some twenty years and outweighed him by eighty pounds of muscle. His salt-and-pepper beard was thicker than the hair on Rendon's head. He wore a battered blue down coat with scuffed patches at the elbows, and a fur-lined leather cap covered his head. His jeans were faded sky-blue and had started to come apart slightly at the knees. A little hint of dingy off-white thermal material showed through. "You said you were bringing somebody in charge."

"Amalia Rendon," she said, stepping forward and offering a handshake. "Sergeant Amalia Rendon, if you like, of the National Elite Interagency Wildland Rapid Response Strike Force. The Firestormers."

"Never heard of you," the bearded man said, barely flicking his eyes sideways at her. He addressed his next question to Edwards. "National agency? You didn't say you were feds."

"We work for the Forest Service," Edwards stammered out. He tried to subtly back up to physically defer to Sergeant Rendon.

"What are you doing out here?" one of the other men asked.

"We'd love to know the same thing about you," Rendon said, trying to phrase that in a friendly tone. "But that can be a story for another time. Did you know you have about eleven thousand acres of fire coming your way?"

The big man frowned and looked up at the sky, which was barely any visible through the trees. "We thought the clouds were acting a little funny. How many acres you say?"

"Eleven thousand," Rendon said. "And counting."

The big man grunted. Behind him, the others shifted their feet and frowned at each other. Rendon eventually gave up waiting for them to say something.

"I didn't catch your name," she said, looking the leader in the eyes.

"Stoyko," he said. "Peter Stoyko."

"Never heard of you," she said back with a grin. It had no effect. "Listen, Peter, we need to get you people out of here." She nodded past him at the other people watching from a distance. "Is this everyone you've got out here, or are there more spread out?"

"What do you mean get us out of here?" Stoyko grumbled. "We live here."

"Where you live will soon be a boneyard," Sergeant Rendon pointed out. "There's a hundred-foot wall of flame coming this way, and there's nothing between it and here but Douglas fir and ponderosa pine."

"Where are you from?" Stoyko asked but didn't wait for a response. "Wherever it is, we do things differently here. We don't let people take what's ours. We didn't roll over for that logging company back in ninety-six, and we're not letting the federal government come in here and run us out either."

"She's trying to help you, man," Edwards piped up.

"This isn't about wanting your land, Mister Stoyko," Rendon explained. "Fifteen minutes ago we had no idea you were even out here."

"That's how we like it."

"But we've got a job to do," Rendon pressed on. "There's a fire coming, and we need to dig a line right through here to try to contain it. This streambed would make a pretty great fire break, actually, if we could clear it."

"Nope," Stoyko said.

"Nope?" Sergeant Rendon repeated. "That's it? Just nope?"

"You got jobs to do, but we got lives to live after you're done. You want to cut some lines through these woods, but you have no idea what that's going to do to the game we live off of."

"Do you have any idea what a fire's going to do to that game?"

"And now you're talking about practically digging up our front yard. I don't think so. If you've got lines to dig, go dig them someplace else, thank you."

Stoyko didn't flinch as he said that last bit, but the men behind him didn't uniformly share his conviction. The other one who'd spoken did so again now, though he avoided any eye contact with Sergeant Rendon.

"I don't know, Pete," he mumbled. "If the fire's as bad as they say . . ."

"They're some kind of firemen, right?" Stoyko replied. He looked at Rendon and Edwards. "You're firemen?"

"Firefighters," Sergeant Rendon said.

"So go fight it, then," Stoyko said. "We're law-abiding citizens who own property. It's your job to keep that fire away from us, right? So go do it. Get it done. Just leave us out of it."

"What if they can't?" the other man said.

"They're with a federal agency, Mike," Stoyko shot back. "They've obviously got plenty of money. Look at that gizmo on her arm. Look at those fancy glasses and watch the kid's wearing. Listen to those airplanes flying over all day. They can handle it."

Ranger Edwards backed up a step and touched the temple of his safety goggles. Built onto them was a small fiber-optic camera and projector that connected wirelessly to the smart watch on his wrist. Together, they performed much the same function as Rendon's datapad.

"Maybe, they can," Mike said. "But shouldn't we be sure?" He looked at Sergeant Rendon for the first time, then back at Stoyko. "Maybe there's somebody she can call to confirm all this for us. Like her boss or something. I don't know."

"So you won't take my word for it even though I've been staring this fire in the face all day," Rendon asked, "but you'll take it from my boss over the radio?"

"Sounds reasonable to me, Pete," Mike said. The other men mumbled their agreement. "Just to be sure, you know."

"Guys, I'm telling you —"

Sergeant Rendon stopped at a tentative touch on her shoulder from Edwards.

"We're going to have to call Lieutenant Garrett about all this anyway," Edwards pointed out. "We don't have a whole lot of time. Maybe they'll listen to him. Or if not him, then maybe Chief MacElreath."

Sergeant Rendon closed her eyes for a second and took a deep breath. When she opened her eyes again, she had regained composure. She nodded at Edwards and turned back to Stoyko.

"I do have to call in about this," she said. "Whether I end up having to move the lines or whatever, this information's got to work its way back up to Incident Command. But to give them the full picture, I need to look around. I need to know how many people you have here, how spread out you all are, that sort of thing. I have to make a full report. The sooner I can get that done, the sooner we're out of your hair."

Stoyko narrowed his eyes at her and crossed his arms.

"Also, we're a little hungry," she added. The MRE she'd eaten wasn't as filling after a morning of hard work as it might have been.

Stoyko sighed and turned his back on Rendon and Edwards, trudging back toward the village. The other men turned around to go with him.

"Fine," he grumped over his shoulder. "Come on, then. Just make that call soon."

* * *

Stoyko didn't stay with them long. He took them to a modest cabin in the center of the small village and dropped them off with a hard-eyed woman in her twenties named Natalya. He told her to show the two of them around, answer their questions, and then come get him. Before she could protest, he stomped off to go huddle in conversation with the other men once more.

Natalya didn't care for Rendon's presence, if the scowl on her face was any indication, but she took an instant liking to Edwards. When the ranger admitted he hadn't eaten lunch, Natalya disappeared into the cabin and returned with a plate stacked with wedges of flat bread, nuts, and dried fruits. Edwards tucked into it as the tour began, earning himself a disappointed glare when he offered some to Rendon.

The tour didn't actually take very long. There were a dozen cabins spread out in a loose cluster along what had once been the streambed. They were all in decent condition and had been built by hand within just the last couple of decades. Nowhere in evidence were there signs of any modern conveniences, such as plumbing or electricity, even from gas-powered generators. Sergeant Rendon didn't see so much as a mountain bike for getting around. The most modern quality anyone showed out here was their clothes and the way they talked. Natalya also made it a point to be sure Rendon knew the bows and rifles the men used to hunt game were the best and newest their money could buy.

What Natalya refused to speak about was why these people were out here in the first place. They survived on hunting, fishing, and growing meager crops in a sheltered garden. Every once in a blue moon, they trekked to the nearest town — miles and miles away — to trade. They rarely brought back anything other than clothes, hand tools, or the supplies they needed to make ammunition for hunting. As for what, if anything specific, drove them to live so far out here on their own, Natalya remained tight-lipped.

When the tour was over, Natalya told the visitors to wait while she went to find Peter again. Edwards had just finished his bread.

"I'm not sure what to do right now, Edwards," Rendon muttered when the locals were out of earshot. "These survivalist nuts act like they want to get themselves burned up."

"They're not nuts just because they want to live out here by themselves," Edwards replied, looking down at his shoes. "Maybe they're just big fans of Emerson or something."

"Hm," Rendon murmured, skeptically. "'Simplify, simplify, simplify.' That sort of thing?"

"Yeah," Edwards said. "Except, Thoreau said that. Not Emerson."

"That's all well and good," Rendon told him, "but I don't understand why they're digging their heels in when we're here trying to help them."

"We work for the government," Edwards said, shrugging as if that answered everything.

"Right," Rendon said, as if that was her point.

"Well, not everybody's been treated fairly by the government. Some people like to kick up a fuss about that. Others just look for someplace they can live and let live and not be bothered." He shrugged.

"Hm," Rendon said again. Edwards had a point. He had a point, and he knew the difference between Emerson and Thoreau. "You and me should talk more often."

Edwards looked away with a blush and scratched the back of his neck. Rendon couldn't help but notice the dopey grin he tried to hide.

Stoyko came back with some of his cronies in tow. Natalya followed a few paces back. "You ready to make that call yet?" the big man asked.

"Just doing that now," Rendon told him, gesturing with her radio. "Give me a second."

She stepped away and opened a radio link to Lieutenant Garrett back at camp. "Lieutenant, it's Rendon. We've got a problem."

"Yeah, my tablet shows that you and Edwards are off the line," Lieutenant Garrett replied. "What's going on?"

Rendon filled him in as quickly as she could.

"Oh crap," Lieutenant Garrett said when she was finished.

"That's what I said."

"And they don't want to leave?" Garrett asked.

"They're definitely not going to leave just because I told them to."

"So how do you want to play it?" asked the lieutenant. "I can tear them a new one for not listening to you, if you like, but I'm hesitant to just say what I know you've already been telling them. You're their point of contact with us, whether they like it or not. I don't want to undermine your authority with them."

Rendon smiled appreciatively. Lieutenant Garrett was young and hadn't had more than an academic understanding of wildland firefighting before joining the Firestormers. Yes, his appointment as strike team leader had been purely political, but he was a sharp guy.

"I've got an idea," she said. She quickly laid out his part in it and told him what she intended to do after that.

"All right," Garrett said, somewhat dubiously. "Let's hope my acting chops are up to snuff."

"Just channel Sergeant Rodgers when he's talking to you."

The lieutenant chuckled awkwardly at that. Rendon felt that he wasn't telling her something.

"You got it," Garrett said, after a moment.

Rendon broke the connection and walked back over to where Stoyko and the others could hear her.

"Sorry about that," she said. "Federal bureaucracy. You know how it is. You can't go ten feet without jumping through as many hoops."

A couple of the locals nodded knowingly.

"Anyway, they should be able to put me through to the commander in charge of this area," Sergeant Rendon went on. She keyed her radio, said her name, and uttered a string of official-sounding gibberish like she was a soldier in a movie on a classified mission. She finished with, "Come in, command."

"Garrett," the lieutenant said, his voice filled with weary boredom. "What is it now, Rendon?"

"Sir, I have the leader of that local community here with me. I thought maybe you could talk to him."

"Give him the radio," Lieutenant Garrett said.

"Yes, sir."

She passed Stoyko her radio and gave Edwards a flat, even look in response to his expression of complete bafflement.

"Who is this?" Lieutenant Garrett asked.

"Sir, my name's Peter Stoyko," the big man replied. "I'm speaking on behalf of my friends and family out here."

"Great," Garrett said. "You guys aren't a bunch of criminals hiding from the law, are you?"

"No, sir," Stoyko said, blinking in surprise.

"Are you terrorists, running some kind of training camp?"

"I don't even know what that means."

"You're not illegals, are you, hiding out from immigration?"

"No, sir," Stoyko told him. That suggestion, over the others, seemed to offend him.

"Then I don't care what you do," Lieutenant Garrett said. "It's a free country. Now give the radio back to my firefighters."

Frowning and confused, Stoyko looked at the radio a moment then tried to hand it over to Edwards. Edwards, who looked just as confused as Stoyko did, handed the radio back to Rendon.

"Rendon?" Lieutenant Garrett's voice barked over the speaker.

"Sir?" she asked.

"Quit wasting time. Get back to your crew and get your line done."

"But what about these people?" Rendon asked.

"Your problem, not mine. Garrett out."

Lieutenant Garrett broke the connection. Rendon just stared at her radio with blank eyes. When she looked up, Stoyko and the other locals were frowning at her — specifically, at her radio — with troubled expressions.

A few seconds later, her datapad vibrated silently as a text message came in. She glanced at it. "That felt horrible," it read. "Please don't ever ask me to do that again." Sergeant Rendon smothered the urge to grin.

"Well, that wasn't worth much," Stoyko mumbled.

"It's like he didn't even care we're here," the man named Mike added.

"He cares," Edwards said, instinctively coming to his lieutenant's defense. Rendon shot him a look. "He's supposed to, anyway."

"Listen," Rendon said, making herself the voice of reason. "He's behind a desk, shuffling papers and watching things on a computer screen. He doesn't know the situation out here. He doesn't know what you're up against. And honestly, I don't think you do either. Not really. But if you let me, I can show you."

"How?" Mike asked.

"I'm going to take you out to the fire front," Rendon said. "Once you see it for yourselves, you can decide for yourselves what you want to do."

Edwards's eyes turned as wide as saucers, his face paling with shock. "No way Lieutenant Garrett's okay with that," he muttered.

A frown of legitimate frustration darkened Rendon's face. "Garrett made this my problem. This is my solution."

The locals looked back and forth from Edwards to Rendon then turned inward to have a quick conference on the subject. When it broke up, Stoyko stepped forward.

"Tell you what," he began. "We'll let you take us out to see your fire, just so as you can say you did it. It's not going to change anything, though."

"We'll see," Rendon told him. To Edwards, she said, "I need a high vantage inside the fire line. Somewhere with a wide view. Find me one."

Edwards hesitated, cringing under the hard look Rendon was giving him. Fortunately, when he was confused or out of his element, he defaulted to obedience. Holding up his smart watch, he engaged his local area map and scanned through it using the tiny projector built into his goggles.

As Edwards looked for a suitable spot, Peter

Stoyko turned to face Natalya, who'd watched the proceedings with avid interest. He made a vague shooing motion toward her, gesturing for her to go back to where the rest of the community looked on.

"We're going to go take a look at this fire of theirs," he told her. "We'll be back soon. Go tell the rest of them."

Natalya nodded once and dashed over to where the women — and all the rest of the men — waited. She spoke to them rapidly in low tones.

"Got a spot," Edwards said.

Sergeant Rendon came over to him, and he swiped a file from his smart watch to the datapad on her forearm. He spoke as Rendon opened her own map and centered it on the location he'd chosen. "It's about two hundred yards inside the fire line. There's a path up the side of this ridge. I used it to spot for an air tanker run when Raphael's crew first bumped us out here. The Behave software models say we should have plenty of time to get up there, look around, and get back before the fire gets there."

The sophisticated fire-modeling computer program Behave could predict how a wildfire was likely to grow and spread. Incident Command used it to decide how to deploy its strike teams. But the rangers in the field were essential for sending back firsthand data to refine the program's information.

"Looks good," Rendon said. "How long out there?"

"It's about twenty minutes away, if we hurry. I hope these guys are good hikers."

"We ready here?" Stoyko said, coming over to where they were waiting. The four men who made up his little cadre followed him.

Before Rendon could answer, Natalya strolled up beside Stoyko.

"What do you think you're doing?" he asked her.

"I'm going to see the fire," Natalya said, staring up at him defiantly.

"Stay here," he told her. "This could be dangerous."

"I'm going," Natalya replied matter-of-factly.

"We can get six people there as easy as five," Sergeant Rendon said. "As long as we don't waste any more time. Let's go."

With a nudge, she got Ranger Edwards moving and followed him. Natalya fell in right behind them without another word.

Stoyko heaved a sigh and got moving as well, but not before turning to the man next to him and muttering, "Never have kids."

"Don't look at me, bud," the man said. "I warned you."

CHAPTER FOURTEEN

"I warned you," the helicopter pilot told Sergeant Rodgers. "The fire's coming this way. You've got about an hour before this whole area's going to be too hot to stay in."

Miles away from Sergeant Rendon's crew, the search-and-rescue helicopter hovered over a clearing halfway between the Badgers' broken fire line and their buggy. The spot wasn't big enough for the helicopter to land, but it was enough to debark the search team.

As the aircraft hovered, it paid out two lengths of cable from over the doors on each side. Rodgers, Walker, and the rest of the search party clipped carabiners from rappelling harnesses onto those cables.

"We got it," Sergeant Rodgers told the pilot, shouting over the wind through the open door.

"Just keep your eyes on the road, and tell us if they pop out."

The pilot gave a thumbs-up.

Sergeant Rodgers tossed him a quick salute then stepped backward out of the door to the runner, letting the cable take his weight. Beside him, Walker did the same.

With a nod to each other, they leaned out and fast-roped down the cables. Their boots touched ground in seconds. They unclipped, backed off and made room for the rest of the search team.

When everyone was down, Sergeant Rodgers gave the signal on his radio. The helicopter rose immediately, slurping the cables back up like spaghetti. The pilot wished him good luck, and he was off.

The search team consisted of eight people, including Sergeant Rodgers and Ranger Walker. The group's leader was a man ten years younger than Rodgers. When Rodgers stepped up, the man deferred to him.

"Okay, let's spread west," Sergeant Rodgers began. "These woods are full of old deer trails and overgrown logging paths impossible to see from the air. Ethan and his guys could be on any one of them. They've had plenty of time to get past us, so if you find a trail, follow it toward the road, not toward the fire. If you find a sign they've been on it, radio the rest of us. We'll start heading your way. Everybody got each other on GPS?"

The searchers all checked their smartphones and nodded.

"Let's move out."

Sergeant Rodgers and the others peeled off along the search line, putting the direction of the fire on their left. They quickly lost sight of one another in the thick timber and undergrowth, forcing them to rely on radio and GPS to stay in contact. Rodgers and Walker took the last leg, with Rodgers moving out to the farthest position.

When they were all in position, their search line drew a broad arc out in front of the fire line.

Years ago, Sergeant Rodgers had hiked and camped in these woods, but today they barely resembled the forests of his youth. The fire made the biggest difference, of course. The wind carried smoke in along the ground, making the place resemble some haunted moor. The trees had transformed into dried skeletons as the heat sucked the moisture out of them.

Even at this distance from the actual fire, its heat was oppressive in the muggy summer afternoon. The wind kicked up dirt and leaves and occasionally flicked around brightly glowing ember specks. The landscape was the same, but it was as if Rodgers were remembering it in the grip of a nightmare. The eerie blowing of the wind and the distant roar of the fire heightened that sensation.

As Sergeant Rodgers pushed ahead through the undergrowth, he made a few attempts to reach his brother. The only response he got back on the radio on the Badgers' frequency was static.

He tried Ethan's cell phone, but it went straight to voicemail. Firefighters weren't supposed to use their cell phones on an incident site, but most firemen who had them carried them in case they needed to make job-related calls. Ethan's was apparently off, and Rodgers didn't know anyone else on his crew.

In a moment of inspiration, he radioed the rest of the search team to see if anyone else did. They didn't, so Rodgers sent a request up the chain to Michael Farrant back at Incident Command to get a list of their cell numbers.

If he and the search team couldn't raise the Badgers by radio, maybe at least one of them would have better luck by phone. Reception was dodgy out here, but there was coverage. Farrant told Rodgers he'd get right on it and get back to them.

Before that inquiry yielded results, Sergeant Rodgers stumbled onto a path. It wasn't wide enough to be visible from the air, but it was wide enough for two people, shoulder to shoulder.

He pushed out of the brush screening it from one side and gave it a good hard look. It ran east to west, parallel to the search line, and showed signs. The marks on the ground signaled that something heavy was being dragged.

Sergeant Rodgers followed the path a bit back toward Ranger Walker's direction and found confirmation that *someone* had been here: a fresh boot print in a patch of soft earth. It was the right size and shape of a logging boot just like the kind Rodgers and most of the other wildland firefighters wore.

The only thing was, it was facing west, heading outside the search perimeter. The way the path curved, it was moving away from the direction of the road and the buggy.

"This is Search One," Rodgers said to the rest

of the team over the radio. "I've got something. Tracks leading west on a fresh path at my location. Anybody else see anything?"

A chorus of negatives came back.

Walker added, "West? You sure it's them, Sergeant?"

"Not a hundred percent," Sergeant Rodgers replied. "It's possible, though."

"Why would they be going west?"

"I don't know." Rodgers sighed. "It doesn't make sense. But nothing else about this makes any sense either."

"Should we form up on you?" the search-and-rescue leader asked.

"No," Rodgers said. "Keep up the sweep in case I'm reading this wrong. I'll play the path out a little while."

"We don't have much time," Walker pointed out. "Fire's coming."

Sergeant Rodgers checked the real-time fire map on his datapad. Walker was right, as if the ever-increasing roar of the fire behind him wasn't enough indication.

"I'll be quick. Just let me know if you guys find a better lead."

"Will do. And you likewise."

Sergeant Rodgers headed off down the path in the wrong direction. As he did, he hoped without hope that his little brother had had more sense than to do the same.

CHAPTER FIFTEEN

As Sergeant Rendon trekked toward the fire overlook, she hoped without hope that Stoyko and his community would come to their senses.

The trek wasn't long as the crow flies, but the thick ground cover and the uneven terrain made it take twice as long as it should have. As the land carried them up higher, the breaks in the trees grew wider, allowing them to see more smoke darkening the skies from the near distance. The roar of the fire came to them as a background whisper that steadily rose in volume. Off to one side, they could hear the faint whine of chain saws where Rendon's crew was still working on the fire line. They left that comforting noise behind and tucked in toward the ever-spreading fire front.

Edwards slowed his ground-eating stride for a bit, falling back to walk beside Rendon. The pair of them were in the lead with the locals strung out behind them in a line. He tugged nervously at the cuffs of his Nomex work shirt, working himself up to say something.

"What is it, Edwards?" Sergeant Rendon asked him, keeping her voice low.

"Just wanted to tell you," he began, looking everywhere but at her. "Just wanted you to know I'm sorry about back there. What I said."

"About what?"

"About the lieutenant not being okay with this," Walker continued. "I saw you talking to him by yourself. I should have figured you were up to something. I didn't mean to undermine you. I hope I didn't mess things up."

"You're fine," Sergeant Rendon told him, trying not to laugh in the face of his uncomfortable sincerity. "I got these guys right where I want 'em. We're nearly there, right?"

Ranger Edwards checked his watch. "Yeah, it's just up here." He glanced up into the projection field on his goggles. "Fire's coming on fast. We'd better hustle."

The ranger jogged back up into the lead, and Rendon looked back over her shoulder to relay Edwards's update to the others. They tightened up their line just in time to huff and haul themselves up the tricky goat path that led up the last ridge to the vantage Edwards had chosen.

One by one, they came around a boulder at the top, held in place by the roots of an old tree onto an overlook with a sheer drop on the other side. There they beheld the immensity of the fire spread out across the foothills.

"Holy cow . . ." Natalya gasped.

Below them, the landscape resembled a war zone. A fleet of planes and helicopters buzzed back and forth over the area, all under the coordination of the Air Operations branch back at Incident Command. The planes — enormous air tankers — swooped low over the ground releasing ten-thousand-gallon payloads of fire-retardant chemicals. The choppers were even more precise, dropping smaller payloads on specific targets from internal tanks and from collapsible two-thousand-gallon buckets.

The sky above the aircraft fire retardants belonged to a smaller unit of just a handful of planes and helicopters. These were the spotters and the search-and-rescue craft that acted as Incident Command's eyes in the sky.

As impressive as the air show was, however,

it paled in comparison to what was happening on the ground. The fire had come closer to the ridge than Walker had predicted, affording the onlookers a better-than-expected view of it. Searing orange fingers clawed their way across exposed overgrowth as if to drag the fire bodily behind them. The heat from them was so intense that even the ground that wasn't actively burning steamed and smoldered toward the ignition point. The land seemed to be boiling away from within.

Where trees stood outside the fire front, the scene was even more dire. As thin, sinister tendrils of the fire crept or raced along the ground between them, the trees seemed to shudder in terror. Hot embers carried on the wind tore bright orange holes in their canopies right before the witnesses' eyes. Smoke began to rise on the side of the bark closest to the fire. Sap in the trees' veins bubbled and expanded like water in a kettle on the stove. All across the fire line, Rendon could see spots where escaping sap bubbled and ran down the trees' skin like wounds. And that was only where that boiling sap could find some way to escape the tree. Where it couldn't . . .

"Look right down there," Rendon said, pointing at a thick knot of pines just ahead of the fire front at the base of a hill. All of the trees there were smoking, but on none of them could she see sap running. That meant the pressure inside at least some of them was building . . . building . . . building . . .

With a thunderclap that made Edwards jump, one of the trees in the center exploded as the trapped, boiling sap tore it apart from the inside. Before any of the locals could say anything, another blew. The fire was in among the trees on the ground now, and in just a matter of seconds, it took hold of them. Winding up the trunks, the flame torched up all the way into the canopy, turning the ruined knot of seventy-foot trees into a towering wall of hundred-foot-tall flames.

"Good lord," Peter Stoyko whispered.

The look of horror on his face said it all. The knot of trees the explosions had come from represented in miniature the magnitude of the rest of the blaze they were staring at. The interior was completely lost in a mountain of black smoke turning to thick gray as it pierced the sky. The true center closest to the ignition point was impossible to see, but the expanding outer core was a nightmare of living flames. They gnawed on the remaining tree trunks and greedily flowed outward to fill any space along the topography that their initial mad rush had left unburned. In places where the trunks, the understory, and the canopy of the forest were fully involved, the flames roared like on the surface of the sun.

The fire played havoc with the weather as well. As it created unimaginable heat, the air it heated shot skyward carrying the smoke and creating convection currents. The cooler air around the fire was sucked in to replace the rising hot air, giving birth to constant winds that blew in around the fire. The tallest of the blazes danced in the winds like monsters.

"Look," Rendon said, pointing into a different section, closer to the heart of the fire. She practically had to shout to be heard over the roar of wind and flame. "That's what we're up against down there. Watch."

Before the locals' horrified eyes, the wind whipped and warped the flames on an isolated stand of spruce into a tornado of fire. The twister danced through the trees, sealing their doom as it caught them all ablaze one by one. Two of them exploded into burning chunks in the thirty seconds the terrifying scene took before billowing smoke covered it.

"You're fighting that?" Natalya asked, her eyes wide, almost to the point of being in shock.

"Yeah," Sergeant Rendon told her, told them all. "My team's back there right now digging out a defensive barrier with a bunch of chain saws and hand tools."

"You can't put that out," Peter Stoyko said, his eyes as wide as his daughter's.

"We're not here to put it out," Rendon explained. "We're just trying to stop it so it doesn't eat up this whole place. What you've got to ask yourself now, is what happens if we can't. Your homes are right where our fire lines need to go to contain this. We can adjust inward a little, but you know this forest better than we do. What if it's harder to move through than we expect? One shift in this wind can push that fire up on us fast. If we're digging out in front of your houses, do you really still want to be in them if we have to fall back and abandon the area?"

"No," Stoyko said. His voice was so soft his words were nearly lost. "We've seen enough. We should get back. We need to get ready to leave."

* * *

The scene that greeted them when they got back to Stoyko's village was a surprise to all the local men, though not to Natalya. Edwards looked just as shocked as the men did. Rendon less so.

Everyone still in the village was waiting by the stones that split the streambed, dressed for a hike and carrying knapsacks bulging with supplies. They were as laden with gear and provisions as the Firestormers had been when they'd first hiked out to the line. Even the children not small enough to need to be carried themselves were lugging small patched-up sacks.

"What's this now?" Stoyko said, taking the scene in. He looked at Natalya.

"I told them you said we needed to be ready to go by the time you got back," Natalya said, daring him with her eyes to reprimand her for it. "Momma took care of it."

"You're in big trouble, young lady," he grumbled at her. She grinned.

"All right, everyone," Rendon said, stepping up to address the crowd. "You've got a long way to go." She gestured to her ranger, standing behind her. "This is Corey Edwards. I'm going to need you to follow him and do your level best to keep up. You've got a long way to go and not much time to get there. Edwards will be at the end of the line making sure no stragglers get lost."

"Sounds fine to me," Edwards said, stepping up beside her but speaking quietly just to her. "But where am I taking them?"

"Camp first," Rendon said. "Let them rest, get them fed, then take them back to where we parked the buggies. Lieutenant Garrett's got some Red Cross volunteers on the way there to pick them up."

"Already?"

"Of course," Rendon said with a wink. "What do you think I was talking to him about for so long before I made him pretend to be a jerk in front of everybody?"

Edwards grinned. "You're lucky Mister Stoyko over there isn't as stubborn as I thought he was."

"Nobody's so stubborn he'll put his whole community at risk just so he doesn't have to take orders from me," Rendon said.

"Speaking of . . ."

As the villagers began to gather around, Peter Stoyko came up to Rendon with Natalya in tow. He looked down at Rendon with blank, hooded eyes. Rendon nodded for Edwards to go ahead and get people ready to move. He did so.

"Where are we headed?" Stoyko asked.

Rendon told him the plan.

"Hm. Your lieutenant's not going to be too happy to see us all."

"I'll handle him," Rendon said. "He's much nicer in person than on the radio."

"What happens once we're out of the way?"

"We're still sorting that out," Rendon admitted, "but we've got the Red Cross on it. They'll be able to get you someplace comfortable pretty quickly. They'll be able to let you know how soon you can get back to your homes."

"If we can," Stoyko said.

Rendon frowned. "That's fair. You've seen what we're up against. I can't make you any promises — this business is too unpredictable for that — but let me tell you this . . . We're going to do everything we can to keep this fire from getting anywhere near your homes. This is our top priority now. We're going to do everything we can for you. If there's anybody out here working this fire who can save your village, it's us."

"I hope you're right," Stoyko replied glumly. "We'll see." He turned away, paused, then turned back once more. "Hey, what'd you say your name was?"

"Amalia. Amalia Rendon. Sergeant Amalia Rendon, if you like."

"You're all right, Sergeant," Stoyko told her. "For a fed, anyways."

"You too, Peter," Rendon said. "For a bull-headed mountain man."

Stoyko grunted and gave her the barest hint of a smile before turning away with his daughter and joining the others forming up around Edwards. As the long procession out of the village began, Rendon keyed Lieutenant Garrett on the radio.

"Lieutenant, this is Rendon," she said.

"I read you," he replied. "Did it work?"

"It worked. They're on the move," Rendon responded. "I'm heading back to the fire line to help out my crew."

"Good work, Sergeant," said Garrett. "Hope to see you soon."

Rendon snorted a little laugh. "From the looks of this thing, sir, I wouldn't count on that."

CHAPTER SIXTEEN

"From the looks of this thing, I wouldn't count on it," Chief MacElreath told her husband. Then she hung up the phone inside Incident Command, knowing that the actual chance of her making it home for dinner was slim to none.

As day became night, Chief MacElreath and her staff worked tirelessly, but the fire was finally nearing containment. If they could lock its two longest fingers down, the possibility of this blaze growing out of control would be a lot less scary.

Chief MacElreath had kept her Firestormers on the line, but she knew that they were wearing thin. If it weren't for her strike team leaders demanding to stay on site as long as humanly possible, MacElreath would have seriously considered letting OpSec pull them out already. But now was the time. If they couldn't get their lines finished soon, they were coming out of there before the fire could trap them inside.

Chief MacElreath sat behind Wilmond High's principal's desk, staring at the monitor of her laptop. She clicked through window after window of reports, topographical maps, fire projections, and a thousand other bits of information she was responsible for sifting through. All around her were stacks upon stacks of paperwork she had to fill out to keep the firefighting effort going. She looked up at the cat poster on the wall exhorting her to "Hang in There!" She sighed.

"Cram it, Morris," she muttered to the poster.

Just then, her office door banged open, and Smalls blew in like a storm front. "We have a problem, boss," she snapped.

Chief MacElreath forced herself to remain calm. "What's up?" she asked, fearing the worst.

Before Smalls answered, she looked back out the doorway and barked, "Get in here!" Chief MacElreath was not pleased to see Topher Smith sidle up beside Smalls in the doorway.

"You're killing me, Smalls," Chief MacElreath groaned. "I don't have time for —"

"Tell her!" Smalls snapped at Smith, pointing at MacElreath. "Tell her what you did."

Chief MacElreath turned serious eyes in Smith's direction. Smith came into the room fidgeting, his expression flickering between smug self-satisfaction and angry defiance.

"You've been ignoring me," he began, glaring at MacElreath. "I tried to tell you about the martens, but you wouldn't listen. Nobody at your agency cares. The more I tried to get your attention, the harder you shut me down. That hatchet job you did on me in the news was the last straw. Well, today I'm going to make you care about the Humboldt marten, Ms. MacElreath."

"It's Chief MacElreath," Smalls barked. Smith flinched. "Get to the point already."

MacElreath knew she hadn't been ignoring him. To be honest, she just had higher-priority problems. Like the community Sergeant Rendon had come upon. The dire circumstances that Sergeant Rodgers and his brother still faced. And the very real possibility that Lieutenant Garrett wasn't capable of dealing with it all.

"I've been reading your progress reports," Smith said. "You've got the fire contained to the north and south, but it's still spreading east and west. You've got almost all your firefighters on the eastern front, but that western front's still moving toward the Humboldts' habitat. Nobody's doing anything about it."

Chief MacElreath took a deep breath. "Sir —"

"Don't," Smith snapped, cutting her off. "I know what you're about to say. That people have to come first. I know that. But I also know there aren't any people out there. It's been evacuated. Empty. So I'm here to let you know what I did to make you care about what's important to me."

"What?" MacElreath asked.

"You remember those fifty-thousand subscribers I have on YouTube? You remember those crusaders I got out here on a day's notice? Well, they weren't my most motivated people. No, there's people like me who really care about humanity's role as stewards of the Earth. Over these last three days, I've convinced a hundred of them to help me get your attention. Right now, they're spreading out into the Humboldts' sanctuary in cars and on foot, right in the path of that fire you don't think is important enough to put out. They're not going anywhere until you stop that fire and save the sanctuary."

The kid's admission hit Chief MacElreath like a punch in the guts. She wanted to bolt angrily to her feet, but she wasn't sure she could trust her legs. Her head spun at the sheer stupidity of what Smith was saying. For long seconds, all she could do was stare Smith in the eye, unable to form words. And yet, gazing into them, Chief MacElreath saw something she didn't expect.

It gave her pause.

"Yeah," Smalls said into the silence that followed. "You see what I mean, boss? Who do you want me to call to pick this punk up — the police or an ambulance?"

Chief MacElreath stood up, slowly, serenely, never taking her eyes off Smith's. She came out from behind his desk and moved to stand in front of the younger man. This close, MacElreath stood over him by several inches. Smith thrust his chin out and glared up at her.

"Samantha, will you give us the room, please?" she said, carefully controlling her voice.

"Oh yeah," Smalls said with glee. To Smith, she whispered, "Nice knowing you, Topher." She left and closed the door behind her with a bang.

Smith took a step back from Chief MacElreath but refused to lower his gaze.

Without a word, MacElreath began to slowly unbutton the cuffs of her long sleeves. The shirt was none too fresh, and she'd long stopped closing the collar button, but at no point since she'd arrived on the scene had she worn anything but long sleeves while she was on duty.

"Hey, I've got my rights," Smith said. "You can't hurt me. I'll sue!"

"Relax," Chief MacElreath said. "You've got Smalls pretty worked up, but I know what's really going on in your head." As she spoke, she began to roll up her sleeves.

"What are you talking about?"

"You're scared," Chief MacElreath said. "You're not scared of Smalls, though all that shows is you don't know her very well. I doubt you're scared of me either, but you are scared. I can see it. And it doesn't go away when you're talking about your martens-with-E's. That's the key, I think. You're actually scared for those animals."

Smith seemed to deflate a little with every word. He sighed and dropped his gaze at last. The kid also unclenched his hands from the fists he'd balled them into.

"Nobody else cares about them," he said, almost too softly for Chief MacElreath to hear.

"Let me show you something," MacElreath said. She'd finished rolling up her sleeves, and she held her forearms out into the light. From her wrists to her elbows, her chocolate-brown skin was marred by gnarled scars that gleamed like wax. Smith's eyes widened. The scars went up past Chief MacElreath's elbows and disappeared up her sleeves. On the left side, they ran all the way up to her shoulder and halfway across her back. "You want to know how I got these?"

"Okay."

"I used to be a smokejumper. The first woman jumper, in fact. Up until the nineties, that is. I was out there on the fire line with one foot in the black, just like my Firestormers are right now. In ninety-seven, my unit dropped in on a chaparral fire up north of Santa Barbara that was eating up everything in sight. We played tug-of-war with it for a few days until it blew up and pushed us all the way back to this old cowboy's ranch out in the middle of nowhere.

"He put us up, fed us, and we did everything we could to keep the fire off his property. He tried to figure out how to get his horses out of there without just turning them loose. Well, time ran out on us. The fire blew up, and it was all we could do to hold the fire back long enough for the rancher and his kids to get out of there. They could have just run for it, but every one of those people who lived on that ranch stayed right up until the last second trying to get those horses out of there. And we did everything we could to give them every second they needed."

"What about the scars?" Smith asked quietly. He hadn't taken his eyes off them.

"Freak dumb accident," Chief MacElreath said. "We were cutting down a stand of trees and didn't realize the wind had kicked some embers into the canopy. The branches started catching fire over our heads, and one of the big ones came down on me. Nobody saw it happen, so it took the guys a little bit to figure out why I'd stopped cussing at them and yelling at them to hurry up. That's what they tell me, anyway. All I know is I heard a huge crack like a gunshot, then I woke up in the hospital."

Chief MacElreath stopped. The time that had followed had been a nightmare. She never told that part of the story. She didn't even like to think about it.

"Anyhow, can you grasp what I'm getting at here?" she concluded.

"Sure," Smith said. "Standard guilt trip. You're saying if I make you move your people and one of them gets hurt, it'll be my fault."

"That's not my point at all," Chief MacElreath replied. "My point is I was on that line because I cared. I wanted to protect those people on that ranch. I wanted to protect the ranch too. Heck, I even wanted to protect the horses. I wanted to save everybody and everything I could from that fire. I feel that way about every fire. Even now — especially now. And my crews out there on those lines, they do too. If I pulled them away and put them in front of your martens, they'd give every last bit of blood and sweat in their bodies to stop that fire. That's what they're out there for. That's why I hired them. So don't come in here saying nobody cares but you. It's our job to care."

Smith dropped his gaze.

"Frankly, I think you believe that's your job too," the Chief went on. "You care about these animals, so you're trying to protect them. But you can't come in here and try to tell me that as much as you care about some endangered species, you care less about your fellow human beings. I barely know you, but even I can tell you're better than that. I don't care how many environmentalists there are in this state, there's no way you'd convince one hundred of them to go play chicken with a wildfire when you weren't even willing to do it yourself. You're not some cult leader. You're just a kid with more good intentions — and more guts — than sense."

Smith sagged and backed up against the door to lean on it like he was the one with any right to be exhausted.

"Fine," he said, "I was bluffing. You got me."

Chief MacElreath relaxed inwardly, staving off a huge sigh of relief only with a massive effort. She'd only been about fifty percent sure the kid was bluffing.

"Topher, you don't realize it yet, but I just did you the biggest favor of your life."

Smith cocked an eyebrow. "How?"

"The fact of the matter is, I just don't have the manpower to spare right now. If I'd believed you about that sanctuary — or if, God help you, you hadn't been lying — and I started pulling crews off, we'd lose Klamath. Today. It wouldn't have been gone by sundown, but it would have been gone by sundown tomorrow. No endangered weasel is worth having that on your conscience for the rest of your life."

Smith didn't say anything. He just shook his head and twisted his face into a frown. Finally, all he could get out was, "This sucks."

"I know," Chief MacElreath said. "But we're not superheroes. All we can do is save everything we can and learn our lessons from what we can't. You don't have to like it — I know I don't — but you do have to accept it. Okay?"

Smith nodded glumly. "I get it. I'll . . . I'll stay out of the way."

"All right, then," Chief MacElreath said. She began rolling her sleeves back down and moved back to her own side of the desk. "I can't promise you we're going to get around to that part of the fire in time, but I give you my word we'll try. As soon as I have the crew freed up, we'll do everything we can for your martens. All right?"

"Fine," Smith said, looking at the floor. He opened the door and paused just long enough at the threshold to say, "Whatever."

And with that, he was gone, leaving Chief MacElreath alone in her office once more. The lights on her multiline phone started blinking, one by one. Her e-mail on her laptop dinged with a new message. Her smartphone vibrated with a new text coming in.

Chief MacElreath sighed and got back to work.

CHAPTER SEVENTEEN

Lieutenant Garrett sighed. "Back to work," he told himself, burying his face in his tablet.

What was supposed to be an eight-hour shift on the line for the Firestormers turned into thirteen, fourteen, and then fifteen. Lieutenant Garrett monitored that effort on his tablet, marveling at the speed with which his plan came together. All of the strike teams made rapid progress, digging their firebreaks without any casualties or wasted efforts. Each team — from elite Firestormers to the local firefighters — traced out its lines perfectly.

They quickly achieved containment around the fire faster than it could advance.

The Firestormers were by far the fastest workers on the blaze. Sergeant Rendon's crew members were the quickest on the line, and Sergeant

Rodgers's were undoubtedly the toughest. That latter quality turned out to be what was most important as day turned to night.

By the end of the hour sixteen, Lieutenant Garrett was ready to call his teams for their evening meal — to be airdropped presently — and a well-deserved sleep shift. Containment efforts were going so well, however, that Chief MacElreath didn't want to slow the pace and potentially give up the advantage. Judging wind and weather patterns, Incident Command called for another three hours on shift to try to sew up the perimeter.

Lieutenant Garrett's crew bosses had each laughed at him over the radio when he'd relayed that information and tried to apologize to them for it. They'd apparently seen the extension coming before the lieutenant had.

When the seventeen-hour mark rolled around and Incident Command had called for another extension, however, the crew bosses' reaction was restrained. Grim even. Their crews had long since eaten their MREs and the energy bars they'd brought along as between-meal snacks. Everyone had been back at least once for more water, and the early afternoon's mad rush of progress along the fire line had slowed to a crawl. The fire was bearing down on the crews along all sides of the fire front, but the containment perimeter was *almost* finished, so Chief MacElreath made the call to keep the crews in place until the job was done. It hadn't been what the weary firefighters wanted to hear, but the crew bosses agreed that it was probably the right call.

The official end of their day came around two o'clock the next morning. One by one, his crew bosses reported in that they'd finished their legs and Richards's and Raphael's crews had already met up at the abandoned quarry.

Lieutenant Garrett reported that information back to Incident Command, but he was so strung out from the day spent coordinating and communicating back and forth that he didn't realize the significance of that development at first. It wasn't until Chief MacElreath got on the radio herself and congratulated him on his job that Garrett realized the job was getting done.

The fire wasn't out — there were still days of work yet to do — but it was nearing containment. No one had lost their lives. No property had been destroyed. The Firestormers' mission was, by all accounts, turning out to be a success.

Only one question remained, and Sergeant Rodgers asked it while he had Lieutenant Garrett on the radio.

"I need permission to backburn this area, Lieutenant," Rodgers told him. "Ethan's out here somewhere, I know it. But I need more time. A backburn could drive the fire away from here."

Lieutenant Garrett shook his head and relayed what Incident Command had told him earlier. "Negative. The wind's not right on our side. Strike Two and Strike Three's lines are upwind, though. They're going to backburn on their side, and the wind should push it around toward us before our finger gets here."

"Yes or no would have been fine." Sergeant Rodgers sighed.

"Fair enough," Garrett said, knowing he didn't have to hold Rodgers's hand like that. "That's a negative. Now get out of there before it's too late. We'll send another team of search-and-rescue choppers after your brother. It's too dangerous to be in there on foot."

The two-way radio began to crackle, and Lieutenant Garrett fiddled with its channel. Then, after a moment, Rodgers's broken voice came through. "Negative," the sergeant responded.

The radio crackled again. "Rodgers," Garrett said into it, "that wasn't a suggestion. That was an order." The lieutenant released the radio's Call switch, but only static came back at him.

"Rodgers!" he shouted into the device. "Rodgers! Get out of there!"

Nothing but static.

CHAPTER EIGHTEEN

Nothing but static.

Then Sergeant Rodgers's two-way radio went silent. He looked at the radio's power light, which usually glowed green. It was black. Dead. Rodgers's had no other way to communicate with the search-and-rescue chopper he'd just sent away. He had no way to evacuate — except on foot.

So Rodgers kept moving. Although he hadn't found any sign as strong as another boot print, evidence still suggested people had moved down this path in this direction as early as this morning.

Sergeant Rodgers pressed on past the twenty-minute mark and neared twenty-five. One by one, the other searchers began to report that they'd reached the road, all without finding anything. Even the chopper pilot had come up empty and added his voice to that of the others urging

Rodgers to pull out and head north. Farrant had come through eventually with the Hotshots' personal cell numbers, but no one had been able to reach them.

As time ticked down, things were looking grim.

At the half-hour mark after finding the path, Rodgers had almost given up when he heard the faint hint of a sound up ahead. It was a pair of voices. He couldn't recognize them at this distance, but he didn't have to. With new hope swelling, Rodgers took off at a run.

Rounding a bend, Rodgers broke into a shadowy glade where ten sweaty, tired men and women were arguing with a figure in the center. As one, they stopped when Rodgers appeared.

"What the heck are you doing here?" the figure in the center of the group demanded.

It was Ethan.

"I'm looking for you!" Rodgers snapped back. "Why aren't you answering your radio?"

Ethan shook his head and slapped the radio holstered on his belt. "We can't get a signal out."

"What about your phones? I've been trying to call you for an hour. All of you guys."

"They're at camp," one of the other Hotshots said, glaring at Ethan, his flailing leader.

"Your camp's gone," Rodgers reported. "What happened?"

Ethan shook his head and sighed. His face was grimy and blackened with soot. Rodgers had never seen him look so exhausted and weak. A part of him wanted to just scoop him up and hug him right there in front of everybody. He somehow doubted that would have been especially helpful.

"We had a spot fire," Ethan said. "It blew up — fast. By the time we had everybody up and out of harm's way, we couldn't get a line around it fast enough to contain it."

"Okay, I get why you didn't call that in, but why didn't you go back to your buggy?"

"What do you think we're trying to do?" Ethan replied hotly.

"This isn't the way there."

"Yeah, look, the fire cut us off from our escape route, so we were heading to Flatt Ridge to get back onto the road."

"Flatt Ridge?" Rodgers asked, puzzled. "That's five miles back in the other direction."

"I told you we were going the wrong way!" the Hotshot who'd spoken earlier crowed.

Rodgers and Ethan both whipped a glare of death at him and barked, "Shut up!"

He did.

Rodgers brought up a map on his datapad and showed it to Ethan. "Look, *this* is where we are. Here's your campsite. Here's the road where your buggy's parked. *This* is Flatt Ridge."

Ethan went pale. "But I thought . . . I mean . . . We hiked on this path before. I remember it."

Rodgers shook his head, feeling his brother's pain and confusion in his own guts. "Not this path, man. This wasn't here when we were kids. I don't know where this even goes."

Ethan wavered slightly on his feet as the enormity of his mistake sank in. He looked up at Rodgers, and for a moment all Rodgers could see was the little seven-year-old kid who'd broken Dad's car windshield with a baseball.

"What do we —"

A tremendous explosive *CRACK!* cut off Ethan's question. Rodgers flinched, remembering too many bad times in the Marines. It took him a second to realize what had happened. As the fire drew closer, it was heating up the sap in the trees in its path. That sap bubbled and boiled in its veins, and when it couldn't get out of the tree fast enough, it simply tore the tree apart from the inside. Before Rodgers could even process that realization, another tree exploded somewhere back along the path. A hot, strong wind stirred the smoke and underbrush around them, carrying fat flakes of ash.

"We need to move," Sergeant Rodgers ordered. "That fire's right on top of us." He checked the real-time fire map for confirmation. A finger of the fire had raced out ahead of the rest and now lay across the path back the way he'd come. They couldn't go back that way. He told Ethan.

"We'll just have to cut north," Ethan said. "Straight overland, back to the road."

"Look," Rodgers said, showing him the map. "We can't go that way. It's all uphill from here, and it gets too steep just before the road. If this wind keeps up, it's going to blow the fire right on top of us up there. We're going to have to go around to the northwest here."

"We can't get back to the road that way," Ethan said.

"No, but look, there's a big meadow down on this side. It's big enough for a helicopter." Rodgers grabbed the two-way radio on his belt. "Oh . . . right," he muttered to himself.

CHAPTER NINETEEN

Lieutenant Garrett passed the news on to the other bosses and then let Incident Command know his people were on the way back. It actually took him another moment to remember that his rangers weren't in direct contact with the bosses by radio. Raphael's and Richards's rangers were already with their respective crew bosses, but Rodgers's ranger, Walker, was still in the field.

Rodgers's radio wasn't responding, but maybe Walker's communicator was still functional. When he reached Walker, Garrett realized he had a problem. Rodgers and Walker weren't together.

At the same time, Rendon's team was just returning, dragging their tools behind them and shambling like the walking wounded. Lieutenant Garrett directed them to the feast that Incident Command had airdropped.

As they started eating, Lieutenant Garrett checked his tablet to monitor the other crews' progress back to camp. He got good readings from the GPS transponders in his crew bosses' datapads and the rangers' smart watches, but what those readings told him was troubling. Sergeant Rodgers was still where he had been when Garrett lost contact.

"What is it?" Sergeant Rendon asked, noticing Garrett's expression. She drifted over to him with a foil-wrapped hoagie in each hand. One of them was already open and half eaten. Before the lieutenant could answer her, she let out a thunderous belch and leaned back into the sandwich like a starving woman.

"Rodgers is lollygagging," Lieutenant Garrett said, trying to ignore the heavy stench of onions on Rendon's breath.

"He doesn't strike me as the lollygagging type," Rendon pointed out around another bite. Her first hoagie was almost gone already.

"Me either," he agreed. "Something's wrong. Is Edwards still awake?"

Rendon glanced over her shoulder to where the Ranger Edwards was sitting. He had arrived back at camp earlier, with Peter Stoyko and his community in tow. Edwards was chatting them up and feeding them, making them feel comfortable for the moment. As he did, Edwards sucked down egg drop soup from a Styrofoam cup, his first meal in more than twelve hours.

"For the moment," she said.

Lieutenant Garrett's frown deepened. "Tell him to refill his bladder bag and bring it to me."

Rendon didn't question. Finishing off the last bite of her first hoagie and tearing into the foil around the second, she walked over to do as Garrett had asked. Edwards got up, tossed his empty cup in the camp trash bin and retrieved his bladder bag from where he'd stowed it.

Meanwhile, Lieutenant Garrett called Rodgers again on the radio. There was no answer. His worry mounting, he called Walker again.

"Sir?" Walker responded.

"Tell me Rodgers has linked up with you," Lieutenant Garrett prompted.

Walker's reply was much more awake — and alarmed. "That's a negative. We're still waiting for him. Is he having trouble with that spot fire?"

"I called him off. Now he's not responding."

Now Walker's voice was flat, calm, controlled. "Tell me where. We'll go check on him."

"No," Lieutenant Garrett said. "Sit tight."

Sergeant Rendon returned with her ranger's refilled bladder bag on one shoulder just as Walker was replying in protest.

"I caught the last part of that," she said. "Heath's missing?"

Lieutenant Garrett nodded. "He went after his brother. Alone."

Rendon shook her head and then hefted the ranger's bladder bag on her shoulder. "Is that why you want this? Are you planning to go down the line and look for him?"

"I am."

"Lieutenant, we can't just sit tight with a man missing," Walker said over the radio. "You can't expect us —"

"Negative!" Lieutenant Garrett snapped back over the channel. "You guys are sleep-deprived and worn down to the bone. I'm not letting you go stumbling over the line in the dark with that fire bearing down on you. Your orders are to wait right there. You read me?"

It took a few long, tense seconds before Walker finally said, "I read you."

"Good. Now stay put and await further orders."

"That's the right call," Rendon said as Garrett

reached for the shoulder strap of the bladder bag. She gave it to him reluctantly. "But are you seriously planning to go out there on your own?"

"I am," the lieutenant said again. "I've still got Rodgers's GPS on my tablet. I can go right to him faster than I can talk Walker's team to his position and wait for them to look around in the dark."

"It's miles down that line," Rendon said. "And I know you're tired."

"I've still got some gas in the tank," Garrett said, swallowing a yawn that threatened to undermine his point. He shrugged into the bladder bag and fumbled with resizing the straps. "Besides, I'm not as wiped as you are."

"That leg of the line is out ahead of the fire front," Rendon said, "but the fire's been picking up speed all day. By the time you run down to where Rodgers is, the blaze is going to be right on top of you. You're not going to have any time even if you know exactly where to go."

"Sure," Garrett told her, "but I'm a firefighter. Danger's part of the job. Besides, what if Rodgers is hurt out there? I'm the only one who knows exactly where he is. He's counting on me."

"We're all counting on you," Rendon said. "We have been all day — but counting on you to keep your wits and think like a leader. Before you go rushing off into the dark like you just told Walker not to do, ask yourself if that's what's best for Rodgers. If he is hurt and does need help, is your running off on foot the best way to get it to him?"

Before Rendon even finished speaking, Lieutenant Garrett had realized she was right. He wasn't thinking; he was letting himself get wrapped up in the moment. He was getting stars in his eyes, seeing this as his big opportunity to prove himself worthy of his Firestormers' respect once and for all.

But that wasn't his job.

"You're right," he said. "That wouldn't help. This will . . ." He switched channels on his radio back to Incident Command. "Command," he said. "I've got a crew boss down in the field, inside the fire line. His transponder's not moving, and he isn't responding to his radio. I need additional air search-and-rescue units. Now."

"You got it," the captain in charge of the Operations Section said. There was a brief pause, and then he added, "Choppers are already in the air. Shoot me your guy's GPS."

Lieutenant Garrett handed Rendon his radio, held up his datapad and sent Rodgers's

GPS coordinates and transponder frequency information up the chain of communication. The captain, the lieutenant knew, would pass it over to the chief of his Air Ops branch, who would relay it to the search-and-rescue helicopter pilots.

Garrett took the radio back from Rendon. "Okay, they know where he is," he told her. "Now we just have to wait."

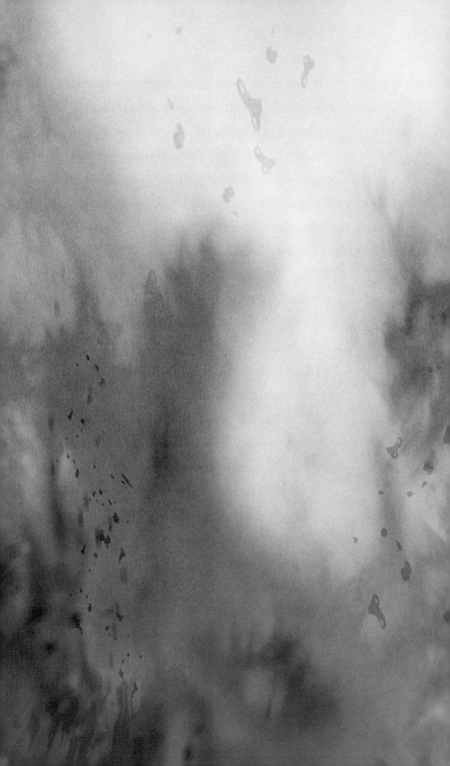

CHAPTER TWENTY

"There's no sense waiting here," Sergeant Rodgers told Ethan and the other Hotshots. They looked to him for leadership now, which earned him a glare from Ethan. "Let's go."

Rodgers headed out at a brisk jog, pushing back into the underbrush. It was hard going, but the rising smoke and heat forced them onward.

The Badgers were tough, as all Hotshots must be, so they made good time away from the fire front. None of them complained about the pace, despite a whole day of wandering. They forced their way through the trackless woods, winding around the steep hills that stood in their way.

Eventually, the trees thinned out and gave way to tall grass and high weeds. The firefighters emerged into the sunlight and took in the view. The meadow wasn't quite as big as it had seemed on Rodgers's map. Bordered by a steep rocky ridge on the far side, a dry streambed to the east, and trees to the west and south, it wasn't much bigger than half a football field. It was open, sure, and wide enough for choppers, but it wasn't much protection from the oncoming fire.

"What now, Heath?" Ethan said, peering over his shoulder.

"We wait," Rodgers replied.

"For what?!" Ethan exclaimed. "We don't have any way to communicate with search and rescue."

"That doesn't mean they don't know we're here," said Rodgers. He placed a firm hand on his brother's shoulder. "When one thing breaks, you don't give up on everything else."

Other Hotshots looked on in awkward silence.

"Ahem!" Rodgers cleared his throat and released his grip on Ethan's shoulder. "I mean, trust the system, kid. It's there for a reason."

"Well, the fire's getting awfully close."

"We'll be okay," Rodgers assured him. It didn't have the comforting ring of older-brother authority Ian's voice would have had.

Ethan sighed and looked at his Hotshots. They huddled together in the grass to rest. None of them seemed eager to meet Ethan's gaze.

"This is all my fault," he said softly. "I screwed this up pretty bad."

"You made some bad calls," Sergeant Rodgers said. "You set your camp —"

"Too close to the fire. I know."

"Your escape route to your buggy's a shambles. Plus you let yourself get turned around."

"This is a bad pep talk," Ethan said.

Sergeant Rodgers gave him a wry smile.

"This isn't all on you," he allowed. "If your guys had better gear, you wouldn't have had so many problems. At the very least, we could have gotten to you last night when you needed help."

"I guess." He sighed again and sat down on the ground. Rodgers squatted beside him. "Looks like you were right. I wouldn't have made a very good Firestormer. Your chief told me you said so. Thanks for that, by the way."

Rodgers closed his eyes. *Now* Ethan wanted to talk about this? "Look, Ethan —"

"No," Ethan said. "You were right. I've been salty about it for a while, but I don't have much room to argue with you anymore, do I?"

"Listen, you've still got plenty of career left to come back from this," Rodgers said. "This isn't even all that bad. You got a little lost, but you didn't get anybody killed. And you got your fire lines dug faster than anybody I've ever seen. If it weren't for some spots of bad luck, you guys would have the whole thing locked down by now."

"Bad luck, huh?"

Rodgers scoffed. "That's just the nature of the work, man. These fires are like . . . Well, they're like William's kids."

"Huh?"

"They don't do what they're supposed to no matter how much you tell them to."

Ethan chuckled, though a little guiltily.

"You're not the only guy who's ever made a mistake in the field," Rodgers said. "All you can do is learn from it and do better next time. And count your blessings it wasn't worse."

Ethan cocked an eyebrow. "That almost sounds like experience."

"It is," Rodgers admitted. "Just not firefighting experience. Remember how I never tell anybody why I left the Corps? It's that kind of experience."

"Oh. You want to talk about it?"

"It's classified. I could tell you, but then I'd have to kill you."

Ethan huffed. "Jerk."

Rodgers grinned.

"Listen!" Ethan observed as the sound of helicopter rotors thumped in the distance.

"Told you," Rodgers said. "That's our ride."

"What do you suppose Command's going to do with us now?"

"I'm taking you guys back to my camp," Rodgers told him. "I'm sure my lieutenant's going to shuffle your guys in with mine for the time being. He'll divide us up and redeploy us. Some of us will work on our lines up north while the rest of us dig out new ones to get your fire back under control."

"Oh," Ethan said. "I just thought . . ."

"What? Did you think you were going to get benched just because of a little setback? Sorry, kiddo. The fight goes on. At least this way we get to fight it together for a while."

"I guess so," Ethan said. He looked up as the rescue helicopter came into view and began its slow descent. "And, Heath, one more thing before I forget . . ."

"Yeah?"

"The next time your boss asks you if I'm qualified for a job, keep your fat stupid trap shut."

Rodgers smirked. "No guarantees."

CHAPTER
TWENTY-ONE

Lieutenant Garrett thought about the guarantee he'd given Chief MacElreath as her voice came over the two-way radio. *Zero casualties.*

That possibility was looking less likely each passing minute.

"We got him, Garrett," Chief MacElreath said without hesitation.

Lieutenant Garrett let out an unexpected sigh of relief.

"Garrett, do you read?" the chief asked after a moment of silence.

"Oh, yes!" the lieutenant exclaimed. "We read you loud and clear!" He smiled at Sergeant Rendon, standing nearby.

"Are all the rest of the Firestormers in?" asked Chief MacElreath. "You didn't send them out to fetch Rodgers, did you?"

"No, ma'am. Just the opposite."

"Good, good. I know Rendon's got more sense, but any of those other knuckleheads would be chomping at the bit to go blundering off in the dark."

Sergeant Rendon grinned at that. The praise seemed to make hours of fatigue melt away, if only for a moment.

"All right, I'll get the chopper pilot on your crew frequency when he's nearing your camp," MacElreath said. "Shouldn't be long. In the meantime, make sure everybody eats, and when the locusts are done, get everybody tucked in. They've earned a rest. That's a good job out there. Over and out."

"Thank you, ma'am," Garrett said, though Chief MacElreath had already cut the connection and couldn't hear him. He realized when he looked up at Rendon that he was grinning just as wide as she was.

"Feels good, right?" she asked.

"Sure does," he said.

Lieutenant Garrett took a deep breath and then cut the connection and checked his tablet to make sure that Rodgers's GPS transponder was actually moving back toward camp.

It was.

Just then, another call came over the two-way. It was one of the search-and-rescue choppers that Lieutenant Garrett could already hear thumping in the distance.

"Thanks for the ride," Sergeant Rodgers said on the other end.

"You're going to have to thank more people than me," the lieutenant told him.

Rodgers grunted. "Ha. Thank the system, right?" He hesitated and then, "But you're the one at the controls. And you deserve to be."

"When I talk sense, people listen," Lieutenant Garrett said, finally knowing what it felt like to mean that.

"*When* you talk sense," Rodger replied, and couldn't help but add, "And that ain't often."

"Okay, wise guy, reel in," Garrett told him. "Your dinner's getting cold."

"Yes, sir — I mean, yes, Lieutenant," Rodger said, signing off.

"I'd say that went well," Lieutenant Garrett said. He lowered his tablet and walked with Sergeant Rendon back over toward the food that Incident Command's logistics people had airdropped in.

Rendon was already halfway done with her second hoagie.

"Pretty well," Sergeant Rendon agreed around a mouthful of sandwich.

"And thanks, by the way," Garrett added. "For your advice, I mean. It helped."

Rendon shrugged that off. "Eh, you would have come to the same conclusion on your own before you even made it to the line. All I did was save you a few minutes of jogging. "

"Still, thanks. Now that we're done for the day, I don't mind admitting I was a little nervous about all this."

"You don't say." Rendon smiled.

Garrett laughed.

Rendon turned to face Garrett and put one sweaty, sooty and now grease-stained hand on his shoulder. "Oh, and another thing, Lieutenant," she said, "I've got something to tell you, and I think you're really going to want to hear it. Frankly, after the day you've had, I think you *deserve* to hear it. Ready?"

"I guess."

"You put your bladder bag on upside down."

At the look on Garrett's face, Rendon and everyone in earshot all burst out laughing.

They were still laughing when the search-and-rescue unit called in with good news.

And Lieutenant Jason Garrett laughed right along with them.

CHAPTER TWENTY-TWO

By the end of the next week, the Klamath National Forest fire was contained. Midweek, the weather had turned ugly again and blown the fire up faster than the Behave software had predicted. OpSec hadn't even had time to relate the change in conditions up the chain of command before the fire cinched its fingers around another ten thousand acres of forest.

In the final days, the beaten and bloody Firestormers deployed to new lines and finally stopped the Klamath fire's eastward progress. That had freed up people to take care of the sluggish western fire front and achieve one hundred percent containment at last.

In the weeks ahead, plenty of mop-up work remained, but the most dangerous stage was over. And for the Firestormers, the battle was over too.

At the end of the final night that week, Chief MacElreath showered and changed inside the Wilmond High School locker room. She attended the customary post-containment press briefing alongside Samantha Smalls. As with the initial briefing, this one was largely symbolic. Chief MacElreath had done so many of them that she could practically sleepwalk through it. She pretty much did, simply reading off the statement Smalls had written up for her and giving short, one-sentence answers to the few questions that the small group of local reporters asked.

MacElreath retained the presence of mind to note, however, that Smith wasn't at the briefing. He'd disappeared after his and MacElreath's talk. He hadn't written a blog since.

When the briefing was over, MacElreath headed back toward her office. Smalls walked with her.

"Good job out there, Smalls."

"You too, boss."

"Most of the team is heading to celebrate the containment," Smalls said. "You want to join us?"

Chief MacElreath smiled. Not every chief could walk the fine line of respect and friendship with her crew. She was glad she could. She was glad to have earned the invitation.

"Maybe some other time," MacElreath finally said. "I've got dinner waiting at home. It's probably pretty cold by now." She laughed.

Smalls chuckled, nodded approvingly, and left without another word.

To be honest, Chief MacElreath couldn't bring herself to celebrate — not yet, anyway.

In the end, the Klamath National Forest fire had consumed more than thirty thousand acres. Half the martens' habitat had been lost, along with Peter Stoyko's settlement. But MacElreath hadn't lost a single life — firefighter or civilian. The media would call that a success, for sure.

Chief MacElreath, on the other hand, wasn't so eager to call it that. But she would call it something else, with months of the upcoming fire season still looming on the smoky horizon . . .

This is only the beginning, she thought.

CARL BOWEN

Carl Bowen is a father, husband, and writer living in Lawrenceville, Georgia. He has published a handful of novels, short stories, and comics. Carl has retold *20,000 Leagues Under the Sea* (by Jules Verne), *The Strange Case of Dr. Jekyll and Mr. Hyde* (by Robert Louis Stevenson), *The Jungle Book* (by Rudyard Kipling), "Aladdin and His Wonderful Lamp" (from A Thousand and One Nights), *Julius Caesar* (by William Shakespeare), and *The Murders in the Rue Morgue* (by Edgar Allan Poe). Carl's novel *Shadow Squadron: Elite Infantry* earned a starred review from *Kirkus Book Reviews.*